The M

"I have read many first or early novels that showed the influence of Jack Kerouac and I have often wondered why and if Kerouac was a direct or an indirect influence. Davis, whose second book it is that we are considering, mentions Kerouac so we may safely conclude that the influence is here direct. I bring this up because I always regarded Kerouac as a dull writer and most of those who labored under his influence seldom were much better. But Davis is a happy exception. He is not afraid of writing well and of using narrative strategies that employ artifice and sometimes art, methods that Kerouac rejected. There is the same progression of events that seems artless and the entrances and exits of characters that are often mere names and impinge on the reader's consciousness solely by means of persistence. This is a remarkable novel. It is eminently readable and assured. I recommend it for its own sake and as earnest of what so good a writer must produce in the future." –*BOB WILLIAMS, The Compulsive Reader*

"Prose in modern times suffers greatly from the Hemingway Syndrome. Out are long-winded poetic riffs, in are word economics and short, terse prose— athletic, as was often the word attached to Hemingway's writing. Few contemporary authors are given free reign to express themselves verbally— Dave Eggers, David Foster Wallace, and Jonathan Lethem immediately spring to mind. Editors, publishers, and literary agents, it seems, prefer mind-numbing mediocrity—Dan Brown and Ron McLarty—to thoughtful, poetic prose. Now enter Josh Davis and Pretendgeniuspress, an independent publishing company along the lines of City Lights and Sylvia Beach's legendary Shakespeare & Company, who gambled by publishing *The Muse and The Mechanism* in a time when thoughtful, even artful, literature has become increasingly marginalized...Davis proves an exceptional prose stylist by alternating Hemingway-esque simplicity with Joycean beauty; although his prose manages to rise to great heights, the dichotomy of his simplicity/poetics never lowers itself to artificiality or contrivances, and he somehow, miraculously, avoids slipping into that dreaded state of pretentiousness. Rich and deeply engaging...*The Muse and the Mechanism* excels at extolling the meandering nature of this generation; we are all rolling forward, often constantly wandering into the unknown, armed only with the hindsight of past failures and embarrassments. Our will to overcome our seemingly inherent lack of motivation vaguely lifts us and propels us forward, and it is that dichotomy—the desire to do nothing and everything—that Josh Davis, unlike his contemporaries, who seem to fall short, masterfully displays." *–DAULTON DICKEY, Popmatters*

Vanishing is the Last Art

Vanishing is the Last Art

a novel by

Josh Davis

Pretend Genius Press
London, New York, San Francisco, Seattle, Washington D.C.

www.pretendgenius.com

Published simultaneously in the United States and
Great Britain in 2012
by Pretend Genius Press

ISBN 978-0-9852133-0-5

Thanks to Brian Gilliland, for patiently editing my fractured prose for less than the price of a cup of coffee per day

to Bob Williams, for unmeasureable amounts of moral support

to Jeff and Dana, for putting up with me while putting me up

to Jonah, for trying

and to Sean, for his ineffable kindness, and for somehow mistaking me for Lazarus.

for Jetz.

...and for Posty and Zooey, who will never be old enough to be allowed to read this.

"I'm not sentimental—I'm as romantic as you are. The idea, you know, is that the sentimental person thinks things will last—the romantic person has a desperate confidence that they won't."

-Francis Scott Key Fitzgerald

I. First Breath after Coma.

Past the first blade, into the open schism, staring. All these emerald shafts, like unfocused crystals growing in the wet, black night—they wink at me and stick to my shoes.

At the edge there is only more, and more after that, and after, and so forth until all mathematical impossibilities become painfully obvious, and the great infinity of chalkboards cough up enough dust and attempt to ask its own name.

"…"

I can't tell what it's all thinking. I can't discern red from yellow. I can't distinguish mechanical textural sounds from animal groans.

"Wallgrain," it wants to say.

"I don't believe in you anymore," I tell it. "Go to sleep. I'll bet you're damned good at it."

All this wordless, pictureless, soundlessness—

Vanishing is the last art. You only get one chance at vanishing. I wonder how my editor would handle the finality.

"I'd like the check, please."

"How will you be paying?"

"For the rest of my life."

People come and go and make sound, speaking through hundreds of centuries of evolved speech and thought, and, I swear they express absolutely nothing. I wonder when we'll evolve past eyelids?

Or maybe I am hearing nothing. Or maybe I stopped listening. Or maybe you stopped making sound. I'm staring at blank expressions made in the shadows, inventing my own words, and I want to bite someone else's tongue but I'm afraid to ask.

3

I chew on my own. It tastes like warm copper.

All the machinery in my brain stops.

"Copper?"

"Taste it."

"Copper."

Something in a newborn lake makes a sound like a groaning door, but it's too dark to see. Something is making opening noises, but it's all so invisible.

"Tell them about the basement," it asks.

"It has a door…"

"Does it?"

"I dreamt it had a door, but I hadn't the first clue how to operate the backyard."

I try not making sense, but it doesn't make any sense. I try attaching meaning to the looseleaf rattle of thought, but I can never shake the beat completely. Three-four. Five eight. Six feet, negative one inch. Everything exists in bodies and formulas and scientifically exacting measurements. Everything, but water and smoke. I stand in the spaces in between spaces wondering how to become one or the other.

Time reacts with gravity and funnels water into the earth. Rain progresses. It occurs to me that everything progresses. Right now, I am progressing towards death.

Someone once told me you stop generating new cells at twenty five. I believed them, and have been dying ever since. If someone told me God was a carrot, I would probably believe them as well, because I don't believe in carrots. These things tend to make a bit of sense if you stand at the chalkboard long enough. Like, "when I was younger I used to play the erasers."

People tell me they did things when they were young, as if now they have relegated themselves to simply standing around to explain the passing of time.

Next Halloween, I'm going to go as elapsed-time footage.

It would be more interesting to say, "When I was younger, I did nothing." In fact, it's been over twenty-six years since I've actually done *nothing*.

"When I grow up, I'm going to be a fireman."

"When I die, I'm going to do nothing."

I want my late fees written out on my tombstone. Are you taking this down? I want my library card used as a name tag at a meet and greet for former subatomic particles. I want my Netflix queue donated to starving drug addicts. I want my eyes hung from my first love's Christmas tree, so she will remember me always.

I want my lawn mowed by my own sense of self satisfaction. I want my teeth whitened with irony. I want my clothes dried on a guitar string, mid-song. I want to take all the curtains down and make socks for elephants. I want to smell like ceramic tile, and taste like exploding sulfur handshakes.

I used to wander a park in a city with a girl, chain smoking. Twenty-five years old, and that's all I remember.

I wonder what happened to that girl, that city, that park? I wonder what happened to all that blood rushing out? I wonder how it all ended? I wonder where all combustible youth ends? I wonder where all that softly inhaled post-matter ends?

In the halls of my memory, everything tastes so fucking exquisite you wouldn't believe it. I cannot describe anything, any further, anymore. There is no combination of senses that could ever get you there. I don't believe in heaven, because there is nothing higher than that taste, that sensation.

I've come a long way since that time. I've come eight years.

Eight years, and no matter what I do nothing lives up to the loose rattle of my own memory. Nothing has been discovered; nothing pioneered. Nothing has mattered.

I am haunted. I breathe oxygen. I am made of carbon. I like long walks on the beach, and short plays about suicidal dragonflies.

"Tell me everyone doesn't rattle!"

"Veer Tory test. Deal neon."

"Stop speaking in anagrams. I'm too old for ice cream!"

So what if this is all just the confused jangle of youth? I have pretended to like ice cream all this time, but it has been a dirty fucking lie.

"Tell us more about the door."

"It has narrative powers, but I want everything to have answers."

I can't stand standing.

I want the check. I'm getting out.

I'm lying inside the brain of a shadow puppet, wondering how to climb down. I've lost my fingers, and as a consequence have no grip on reality.

"Waiter? Check, please."

. . . .

II. Pilgrimage.

Sophia and I are driving to California. We left our hearts—and Sophia's three favorite pairs of shoes—in the city. Now, we are driving northeast through Pennsylvania. Now, Ohio. Now, Indiana. Now, we are glaring, sleepy-eyed, through the gloaming deadlights of Chicago. Now, we are passing through the St. Louis Arches in a mid-day haze, and looking up with quasi-passionate awe. Now, Sophia is taking pictures through the car window.

We are, and are not, in Kansas anymore. We are bearing witness to the county's largest free-standing cross. We are collecting a life's supply of hotel towels. We are stopping at numerous gas stations, and spending thousands of dollars on bad coffee, Red Bull, and shot glasses that say "*Route 66*." I am buying a "*Don't Mess with Texas*" t-shirt.

I want to say that we're being filled with America. I want to say the hours of looking out the window into the ever-expanding glory of the great American roadside have changed me. I want to say that we're drinking with hobos in ghost towns, or riding off into the sunset of some fantastically dusty novel. I want to say we are electing the first black conservative feminist Martian to the International House of Pancakes. I want to say something about all these places we're passing as if we're doing something— anything— more than just pass them; as if we're staying long enough to spoon even the smallest mouthful of the infictitious American dream into our expectant, yapping jaws. I want to say a lot of things about a lot of things.

We stop sporadically in random off-ramp hotels outside of larger cities to keep costs down. We eat dinner in front of vending machines.

Sophia is downstairs in the lobby asking for more towels. Everywhere we stop, she asks for towels. I fantasize about the secret nest of towels she must have amassed between here and the city. By now, I figure she's probably accumulated about seven thousand five hundred and sixty four towels. My only hope is that she doesn't decide to use the towels against me. Nothing good could come of that. I figure I can handle at least three thousand four hundred and seventy three towels. But seven thousand five hundred and sixty four? That's just out of the question.

I stand in the bathroom and open a pack of baseball cards that's been living in my left shoe. Its contents smell deliciously like new wax and old bubblegum.

This is the first pack I've opened since we left, and I'm thinking of proposing to it. In sickness and in health, in hotel bathrooms, for better or for worse, for long as you both should desire lucidity, for as long as you both shall live on the run from adulthood. With this Nick Markakis rookie card, I thee wed.

The door creaks, and I casually throw Nick the Stick into the hotel toilet just as Sophia walks through.

"Did you get any towels?" I ask.

"Mmhmmph," she says through the pile.

I suggest we break character and order room service. Sixteen towels move up and down in agreement.

"Hello? Room service? Is it too late? Great. Yeah, ah…it's 301. Yes—Yeah, I'll have three Heinekens and a turkey club, and—here, hold on…"

Sophia breaks free and catches the phone in a slow motion fabric softener commercial. Her hair fans out across the room, and her body blushes under the flickering forty-watt heaven. She orders a garden salad, tuna fish sandwich (hold the tuna), fried apple blossom, side order of onion rings, side of bread sticks and a partridge in a pear tree.

I am looking at Sophia as if she were God's own club sandwich. She's wearing a wet hotel towel over her bathing suit, but it almost doesn't matter. I stroke the base of a nearby lamp and attempt to use all three wishes to grant me the power to see through cotton-blend multi-fibers. Sophia orders the vegetarian lasagna and something called *the double chocolate dream.* She is twenty-two years old and a size two, but is apparently very upset about this. I have to stop my eyes from tunneling straight through the few bare triangles of exposed skin, right into the fiery center of the earth. I resolve, then, to use my fourth wish to cure my childhood fear of heights.

Sophia hangs up and changes in the bathroom. A bottle of red wine sits on the nightstand and stares eagerly at the sweat on my fingertips. I must have drank that much just waiting for her to come back to the room and ignore me. Funny—I don't feel like dancing.

Sophia emerges in a tight pair of doll-sized blue jeans and a bright long-sleeved shirt that highlights far too many of her good features. She sits down Indian-style on the bed with a magazine, and becomes engaged in what must be either a profound series of

9

hunger sighs, or else a very good Meg Ryan impression. I figure she has about five seconds until she either cums magnificently, or else inflates into a balloon and bursts. Should I say something? Maybe she's about to achieve nirvana. Or possibly the Velvet Underground.

I try watching the grain of the wallpaper as it waves about the room like a slow tide. Sophia yawns, morphs into an insect, and crawls unevenly across the ceiling. I should be disturbed, but now I feel like dancing.

There's a knock on the door. I answer the tray and tell it to watch out for the bats. Sophia, meanwhile, becomes pure energy.

All the food in the world spontaneously vaporizes.

"How is it?"

"Mmhmmph," she says through a pile of breadsticks.

Letterman is on. I'm laying next to Sophia on a long king-sized bed, wondering about third world debt and whether or not the snack machine takes dollars. Then she leans over and kisses me.

"I'm not going to sleep with you, Charlie," she says, tugging on my earlobe with her teeth.

"Okay."

"I mean—that doesn't mean we have to stop."

"Okay." Should I have said that with a question mark?

Sophia pulls out a series of large charts and graphs, and points out several no-fly zones.

"What, no Powerpoint presentation?"

"Mmhmmph," she says through the warm flesh on my neck.

10

And in that moment, I know she's forgotten about all those hallways, all those weeks we lost pinning each other down on her bedroom floor, writhing, pulling, scraping, and biting at the air.

Have you forgotten about the madness of your own breath, or how the texture of your own skin can so easily shift from the soft sweetness of a warm shower, to the salty contaminated mess it became when it touched mine? Have you forgotten about dying, about how your breath would reach that pitch that only dogs can hear? How you gasp and pull in oceans? Or how you freeze and disintegrate?

You would shiver for five seconds, twitch twice, and then stop breathing altogether, and I'd start to wonder if your heart had stopped just as you'd spring back to life each time, begging more, becoming more water, more salt, and releasing more carbon dioxide.

Was it that I told you I didn't love you, or that I didn't tell you back I loved you back? Should I have bought the double-layer box of chocolates instead? Did I kill the sport altogether when I didn't resign in a record-breaking multiyear exclusive contract? I couldn't. I was too young, and there was far too much press coverage.

Now, look at you. You're under me again, but this time you're telling me where *not* to go, when to stop, when and how much to tip the waiter, and just when you expect the salt shaker to be emptied and replaced. It's as if you hardly miss the ridiculous wet meat sound our bodies used to make!

I'm looking at that ridiculous little figure of yours, unfurled and begging to quiver, and I'm frozen with fear. Have you noticed my eyes yet? I can't stop staring, no matter how many times you tell me you've

11

already got car insurance. Was your stomach always cut into little tan triangles? Is that the golden ratio? Were your thighs always so petulant?

I don't know why I even came here with you, now, after all of that; after already having had the exquisite pleasure of building and destroying Rome.

I push her away and stare into the black recesses of outer space tucked between her eyelids. "Look—about how long does it usually take you to get off? I mean—by yourself?"

She doesn't pause, "about two seconds."

"Great."

I dive back in. My left hand caresses the fashionably choppy locks of brown hair on the back of her head and makes its way south. I throw suggestive breaths at the edges of all her secret bases. I polish the outline of her no fly zones with my tongue. I finger the air around all her forbidden holy fissures, and softly trace every legal inch of her oversexed twenty-two-year-old frame. Then I stand up.

"I'm going outside for a cigarette. Have fun."

I can hear her breathing rise through the closed door.

The hallway leads straight out. I crawl down several flights of stairs, and contemplate a thin strip of highway breaking through all the smoke and leading away from all this. The cars don't know. The steak houses, pizza parlors and foreign fast food joints don't know.

This cigarette in my hand just doesn't know. I myself don't even pretend to know. I'm farther away from knowing than the birds that live on top of the shoeless telephone wires.

I crawl back upstairs five minutes later. Sophia is rolling around on a pile of freshly-laundered towels.

"Did you have fun?"

"Yes, thank you." She kisses me tenderly for a fraction of a segment of a subdivision of a second.

We watch the rest of *Letterman,* lying on opposite sides of a long king-size bed. I pour half an orange soda into a bottle of tequila, turn it upside down, and zip my eyes shut.

. . . .

We stop for a while at the Grand Canyon. We look at rocks, holes in rocks, sunlight melting rocks, small reptiles hiding in rocks, and all the Japanese tourists taking pictures of each other standing on or over rocks.

A few hours later, we're back on the road for the final leg of the trip.

The temperature display on the dashboard has topped 100° Fahrenheit. We pull over at a rest stop with a conveniently out of order soda machine, and several signs by the bathrooms warning us of scorpion attacks. I take pictures.

We are on the verge of California. Sophia, newly elected patron saint of circumspection, is finally reverting to something resembling a human being. I think I can actually see her lungs beginning to take in air. Her cheeks are getting a little color back, and for a moment I am almost convinced we are of the same species; even the death grip of her right hand on the door handle has relaxed a little.

I push one of the five CDs I own that doesn't completely offend her deepest inner sexually confused vegan feminist lawyer sensibilities into the slot of the car stereo, and turn the volume all the way up to one and a half.

An hour later, the temperature display climbs to 105°. I wonder about sand blindness, and the long-term effect the color orange has on retinas.

The car sputters out for a fraction of a segment of a subdivision of a second. I hold the wheel steady as Sophia resumes her death grip.

"What's going on?"

"Your car is dying," I tell her calmly.

"What?"

"Your car—it's dying."

"Why is my car dying?"

"We're in the middle of the fucking desert in the middle of the fucking summer, and we've been driving, nearly nonstop, for five thousand miles."

"Why is my car dying?"

"I think it's overheating."

"Well, do something Charlie. Fuck, I have to be..."

"I can't do anything. What do you want me to do, pray to AAA? Spit on the engine? Oh, maybe I could *towel* it off..."

"But I have to be in Costa Mesa *tomorrow*..."

"Look, right now I'm more worried about being stranded in the middle of nowhere in this awful fucking heat. Do you see a ramp anywhere?"

"No. There's nothing! Should we pull over? Should I get the map?"

"It might not start again if we pull over. I think we should ride it out until we either find an off-ramp, or explode."

"Explode?"

"It's a figure of speech. We'll be fine."

"*Explode?*"

"We'll be fine. Hand me a towel."

We spot an exit about a mile off. I push the car, but it won't even top fifty anymore. It, and Sophia are sputtering in unison. I begin to wonder if cars have menstrual cycles.

I hold the wheel steady. Half a mile. Quarter mile.

I make the ramp, and slow down as the engine finally dies. We hit the shoulder gliding in neutral.

Sophia turns the loveliest shade of purple and jumps out, hammering at her cell phone.

We are in the dead middle of nowhere. It doesn't take that fraction of a subdivision of a second to realize this, or to start sweating, or for my breathing to seem more like a partner to leather than I can ever remember.

Sophia starts to sputter and weep.

"Come on kiddo, you'll get dehydrated."

"Fuck, Charlie. Now what are we going to do? Where are we? I'm supposed to be at work tomorrow…"

"Hey, calm down. Look—over there. There's a gas station about a mile off. Call whoever you just called back and tell them to meet us there. We can't wait in the middle of nowhere for a tow in this fucking heat."

"Okay…"

"It's okay. Grab that bottle of water. We're going for a little hike."

We hoof it to the gas station and wait in the drink cooler.

Two hours later, a dust-covered character carved out of prospector soap pulls up in an old Ford truck fit to haul away a small European country. Like France.

"You the tow?"

"Mmhmmph."

"Oh, good. You speak Sophia."

We toss our bottled Peruvian mineral water into a grey rubber trash can, and follow him outside.

Leatherface makes room for us in the cab. He drives us back to the car, and within minutes, hooks up all the necessaries and we're off.

We ask him how often he rescues stranded victims of exploding autos, and he answers in a kind, raspy old southern accent, telling us his life story on the way to shop. He tells us about debt and divorce, and two kids and a twelve-step program television movie of the week bum rap charge for second-degree cowboy impersonation. For a minute, I think seriously about ditching Sophia and asking him if he knows a good bar where we can wrangle us up a couple of empty-but-kind-hearted southern belles in nearby imaginary nightclubs.

After an hour of random running around over story-time, and another half hour of pure Arizona silence, John Wayne's third cousin twice-removed drops us off, tips his imaginary hat, and wishes us less adventure. We wish him the same.

The auto shop flutters in and out of focus like a heat mirage. Men six feet taller than us covered in motor oil and alligator scars wander around like devolved Aldous Huxley Epsilons, and nod their heads gravely. We are told the patient will need to be kept overnight, and are allowed to use the phone to dial a nearby rental car dealer, Sophia's rear suspension breaks down, and her headlights cry transmission fluid.

A half-hour later a young man arrives in a neat new air-conditioned car and takes us to his leader.

It turns out we have stalled, he tells us, right on the edge of the Nevada-California line, and Sophia's super-deluxe golden first-class service plan is just enough to get us a free car, and a free night's stay in a nearby swanky casino. A young man in a James Spader mask makes the necessary arrangements.

An hour later, we pull up to one of the gaudiest and most beautifully overdone four-story buildings man ever created. It slithers right out of the Colorado River, stretches wider than anything I've ever seen, and glows with enough wattage to make a Tokyo architect wet. Sophia takes pictures.

"Finally," I say.

"I guess this is okay," Sophia says. "I'll have to call Costa Mesa, and tell them I'll be a day late. You don't think it'll take more than a day, do you?"

"Why, are you planning on turning into a pumpkin?"

"I'm planning on having a job."

"It's good to have goals."

"Mmhmmph!"

We park a mile away, and make the dusty trek to our new neon Valhalla.

Inside, four of my five senses immediately overload and shut down. Ruby, gold, emerald, topaz, and silver lights spin in blinking spirals over singular blinking strands of light. Ephemeral x-patterns, flashing from the floor to the frantic Technicolor glow overhead, beam from billions of rotating dials that hover and taunt us, like exaggerated electronic Sirens in a Homeric science fiction novel.

The people, all sitting on red vinyl chairs, cough, clap, cheer, frown, and morph into mechanical boardwalk arm wrestling machines and cheap electronic fortune tellers. The oldest wander around, seemingly on ether highs, their dusty broken jaw bones slumped open, gasping and overwhelmed. The youngest ride the track of bronzed carpeting back and forth, holding hands with buff stern future alcoholics, and beautiful little childlike vamping vixens in low white blouses and tight bright blue jeans.

Old blind black men ride by on oddly-automated wheelchairs. Old white men dressed in wrinkled VFW uniforms hobble by on aluminum canes.

The blinking frenzied machines all have campy Japanese game show-worthy names: *Mystic Arrow*, *Double Diamond*, *Gold Mountain*, *Yukon Trail*, *Slam Dunk*, *Instant Free Rockin Prince*, and *Super Wild Cash!*

The whole spectacle is an epileptic nightmare. Cheers cascade from the shimmering metal jaws of the slot machines. Buzzers never stop buzzing. Bells never stop ringing. Traffic stops in the jam of handles and spinning cherry clouds.

The seated crowd is tight-jawed, mealy-eyed and stone-faced. Their hands stay folded for centuries, but their thumbs are nervous rodents. I study them as they give away their hands-on-hat tips, tongue flicks, coughs, and beard brushes.

Between all this there are clowns, gold and silver rain beams, frilly-skirted cocktail waitresses with cheap Botox smiles, sullen old cart men, plaster pillars, plastic chandeliers, and an endless ticker tape

18

parade of flashing suggestive slogans like *haywire*, *bonus, leap, party, rich*, and *wild! wild! wild!*

Every word has an exclamation mark and every corner broadcasts more blips and beeps than a NASA control room.

I get a drink while Sophia checks us into a room. I have another.

I watch the people sitting around the tall, thin tables by the bar, and imagine all the ineffable secret strategies they've developed in trans-desert RV trips, or television thefts.

The Doors, The Beatles, and Elvis play nonstop on spinning silver motorcycle stereos.

I walk around. *Famous dragon cat dog frog dolphin eagle seal lizard cougar penguin safari circus jungle American pride black lagoon cherry banana, plum...*

This isn't the adventure I'd imagined when I agreed to cross the country with a the embers of an old flame, but I'll take it. Really, I'd take anything. But this is better than *anything*. This is something unlike anything I've seen. This is sadder, brighter, and more obtuse than any arch, canyon, towel collection, or sadistic take on foreplay.

I head back to the room, pass Sophia, jump the porch rail, and have a cigarette with the Colorado River. The water lights up with street lights, and the spinning neon billboards. The music turns from flip-flop reggae to hard sneaker post-rock.

I'm a little lucid after five rum and Cokes and sixteen cigarettes on an empty stomach. Two small boats drift by without winking or holding hands. Couples walk by in sad single-file lines. Wallets bark at their solemn owners, who will all go hungry. A lone feather falls on the guardrail. I take it inside and give it a proper home in the thin blue straw of my last rum and Coke.

. . . .

Later, still spinning, flashing, chirping, ringing and buzzing, I sit inside a little microbrew in the back and order a turkey club and a red lager.

The casino sounds slowly die out. Here, the tension in the air is built on hundreds of conversations bent into the white noise, and tucked in tight flowery dresses that lean over barstools, smiling shimmering chap-stick smiles. I watch with awe as blonde-on-blondes faint into pale seraphic champagne waves and flowered black backgrounds. I think this must be the nine o'clock show. I make an honest attempt to flirt with my salt and pepper shakers accordingly.

Thick, polished bronze pipelines weave inverted Y patterns overhead. Keno numbers flash, but are ignored.

I am not ignored. One blonde in big fig leaves looks over my way with the cock-eyed intensity of a bemused German Shepard. I put on my favorite Henry Kissinger mask and look back. She watches me, turns into a butterfly, and flies straight into the mouth of a nearby alligator shirt.

I decide that posing must be the new Olympic sport, and that these must be the trial heats.

The contest seems to begin with a shampoo commercial hair flip, and a flicked-on Camel Light. Next, the eyes of each contestant move slightly sideways so as to be able to catch a more panoramic view of the playing field. Following this, the participants yawn and stretch the arches of their backs, while pursing their lips outwards in teams of two. It appears this is a synchronized sport.

Or possibly, it is a triathlon. I look at another girl; I watch the tight geometry of her movements. A single lock of her hair escapes her left earlobe, followed closely by the German Shepard look, and the ceremonial presenting of the teeth.

Finally, a movement is triggered as each participant moves precisely five feet to the right, adjusts the position of their eyes, and aims sixty years of television knowledge at Carson Daly's haircut. Martini glasses are exchanged, and a bizarre sort of little-kid posture is adopted as flat stomachs are pressed outward, so that the peaks at the top and bottom of the athlete's midsections are firmly established.

Further celebrity haircuts are handed out with further martinis. Everyone scatters, and then the whole process is repeated ad infinitum. At halftime, the audience cheers and sings "Happy Birthday."

Peach is the official color of the neo-Olympics, and must be worn on breast, hip, or lips at all times. Cleavage has been named official mascot.

I might be in heaven. It's funnier than I ever imagined, but I'll take it.

. . . .

At dusk the next day, we arrive in Costa Mesa and everything changes.

The beds I slept in on the road beside Sophia's sexually ambiguous hot and cold streaks are exchanged for a thin wool blanket and a less-than

21

cozy spot on the floor. At night, as she crawls into a warm contortion of pillows and padded sheets and quilts, I cower on the ground feeling the cold of the California night tugging hard at my shoulders and ripping through my short hair. My body aches on the hard ground. I turn over, like a dog making its imaginary bed on the floor, a thousand times unsuccessfully.

I can't help thinking about how briefly removed Sophia and I are from the sweeping romance we'd built back in the city. Only a few months ago, we'd been going out, staying in, breaking in tables and couches and counters, and any and all surface and air in between, making each other writhe wickedly with wild flesh dances aimed into the truest center of the madness of pure sex, panting and sweating in oceanic harmony. Her skin would glow with saltwater. Her eyes would roll drunkenly down her spine. Her lips would part as if Moses were present, and her toes would curl like burning bits of paper curl just before they are fully consumed by fire, and left for thin fragile ash to float off into the air, forever.

Now it's as if she's written out a restraining order against me. I'm not to come within a hundred yards of any of her pink parts.

I might care more.

I might care if her personality was still as attractive as the cut of her stomach, or as fetching as the lovely slopes she tucks underneath her newly pretentious law school attire. I might care if I weren't shivering alone on the floor.

The very idea of sex has taken on a hard height of vengeance. Now, I don't want to make her toes curl backwards for the wondrous panting pauses of her breath, or perchance that the soft and tender touch of her small hands post-act might lull me into a loving catsleep. Rather, I want to drive something hard into her the way one might drive a wooden stake into a vampire—to turn it to dust—to make her body a dead, motionless oblivion.

Now, I drink tequila unromantically until I pass out.

. . . .

During the day Sophia is out, and I am left car-less and miles away from anything. She does give me her key, but she also demands that I be there at 5 o'clock sharp each day to let her in.

So I walk.

I walk across the busy Spanish streets, sticking close to the mesh wire wall, headed towards the bookstores, bars, and cinema which make up the only entertainment worth mentioning. And I observe things.

California is in a current state of plexus. Equally coexisting things I have seen:

1. Kick boxers.
2. Christians behind bars, but never in bars.
3. Fashionably tall people in health food stores.
7. Semi-attractive women with otherwise unattractive birthmarks.
8. Blonde children with unironic smiles.
9, 10. Asians. Lots of Asians.
11½. Hispanics on bicycles who know about guitars, but can't play them.
13. Protestors.

The weather here is also at once decidedly unbalanced, and oddly mechanically sound. From 8 a.m. to 1 p.m., it is overcast and a little cold. From 2 p.m. to 6 p.m., it is sunny and warm, and from 7 p.m. on it reverts to partly cloudy and cool.

The formula is sound, so much so that I manage to move through the system without attracting as much as a blink. I try things, like smoking cigarettes in the outdoor areas of restaurants where there is clearly none of the usual evidence of nicotine abusers; butts, trays, coughing, or audible conversation. I light a cigarette as if to introduce myself. No one speaks, but instead everyone stands up and moves their belongings slightly to the left, as if I were merely a tide coming in too close to their beach towels.

I put on dark sunglasses and walk around the beaches with my pale east coast slouch. I look at the fashionably tall women in reclined nylon beach chairs, and I get the sense that I am the only one with eyes. Back home, the male vulture will not leave the female vulture unattended for more than six tenths of a second. Surely, a crowd would gather after five seconds, and in a matter of minutes a circus tent would be erected, and there would be at least fourteen fire eaters, one hundred and forty three circus clowns, and eighty four lion tamers. *At least.*

The bars are empty during the day, and at night there are so many ropes and lines. Ropes! Imagine! There is condescension on the part of the infinite to the mind of man, and that looks like California. When I see ropes and lines I move on, although I am beginning to think they hold their secret meetings in these places. I am beginning to think this entire charade of blank cool is being orchestrated in roped taverns at night. Lessons last an hour, after which the second group is allowed in and briefed. Then the third. One must always wait at the designated lesson area provided on their voter registration card, or else risk being left out of the loop forever.

No one blinks on the streets. No one blinks at stop lights. Cars weave and dodge rudely between the thin white lines of the highway, and no one bangs a horn, or sprouts a finger. In New York, one of these drivers could have fed a modest garden of extended middles, along with a veritable philharmonic of car horns.

Also, Jimmy Buffet is played over outdoor patio speakers without any trace of irony, as if a cheeseburger in paradise is as common as a colonic, Botox injection, or tooth-whitening laser surgery. I am officially afraid for us all.

I am starting to miss rudeness, slanted eyebrows, the ability to shock, pizza that doesn't taste like leather, and the lullish orchestra of car horns that follows a single offender for days—that draws large red A's on car hoods, and incites finger parades as far as the eye can see. I miss the sleazy pick-up artist, the academy award performance of barflowers, and the sweet choking aroma of sixteen kinds of smoke blending into the ineffable potpourri of the east. I miss orange alerts meaning something. I can't believe I just said that, but I do. I miss the toothless, trailer huddled masses. I miss jukeboxes with filthy, vulgar bar-rock. I miss the fear, the stiffness, the pallor, and the knowledge that at least half the other poor bastards in any given room at any given time will be going home tonight with their right hand. I miss grit and impropriety. California, you make me want to wash my hair in tar, have my teeth painted at a

Chinese beauty parlor, and don a proper Brooklyn boom box blasting the fuck out of Public Enemy records against the sweat stream out of the suited, untranquilized masses—thinning hair, semen stains, sullen shoes, deranged eyes, madness—hungry madness—beautifully damned, and archetypally bemused death vultures that hang over us all that we call man, women, husband, wife, sir, madam, doctor, dealer, boss, paperboy, clerk, whore, bastard, junkie, or Mr. President.

. . . .

Today I watch protesters standing outside of Triangle Square holding up signs saying, "Silent vigil to end war."

This bothers me for two reasons:

1. *War* spelled backwards is *raW*, and who in their right mind ever wanted that *1987* comedy classic to end? Didn't James Joyce teach us anything?

2. I thought these people wanted to be *heard*, to have a *voice*.

"Mr. President we just wanted you to know that, zzzzzip…!"

I walk up to one of them, and stomp down hard on his Birkenstocks as he jumps up and screams, "What the hell did you do that for?"

"You're not very dedicated, are you?" I reply.

Later, I come back dressed as someone else.

"Can you tell me how to get to Harbor and Bay Street?"

"Yeah, take a left here, go straight for about…"

"Gotcha!" I yell and run away. Luckily, they can't catch me on account of the bulky signs and expensively inefficient sandals.

I sit and watch the waxing and waning throng from across the street. A hundred and twenty seven news vans drive by without stopping. The group salivates in synchronized turns, but the vans just keep going.

I purchase a large American flag inside the mall and take it to their side along with a sign saying, "supporting your right to be a moron."

They don't seem to like me. One of them says so. I laugh, and yell, "gotcha!" again.

Finally, they construct new signs saying, "Silent vigil to have this fucker sent to a rehabilitation facility" and lots of people stop and drop coins. I use said coins to buy a round of "I'm with stupid" t-shirts at a gag shop in the mall, and I put all of them on and stand around a while longer. When it gets too hot for all the t-shirts, and I finally tire of taking out my insecurities on others, I go to the movies and drink a Coke.

. . . .

The place Sophia and I are staying in is an off-season sublet of a rather strict Christian college.

Drinking is forbidden here. Unmarried couples are forbidden. Smoking cigarettes is forbidden. Wearing white after Labor Day is strictly prohibited. Baseball cards are punishable by fire and brimstone.

I smoke anyway. I smoke just outside the door, just enough inside the gate to still manage to piss off the hierarchy. I smoke, in fact, on the red curb marked "fire zone" because I think I'm being clever. I drink, as well. I hide three bottles of liquor and a couple bottles of wine under the sink. Christians never look under the sink. That's where Jesus hides.

Tomorrow is Sunday, and I'm thinking about getting up early for church. Not that I really want to go to church, but I wouldn't mind watching everyone else going to church. I suppose I'm a Christian too, technically, but I am not a church Christian. If God Almighty is as full of love and benevolence as they say He is, I doubt the man upstairs would really care if I went to church so long as I didn't murder nuns or anything like that. Murdering nuns is frowned upon.

I think I'd like to get a chair to sit in while I'm watching the Christians go to church—maybe a nice little folding beach chair, since we're all so close to the beach. I'd like to sit in my nice bright nylon folding beach chair in the clothes I slept in, and the beard I grew last night. I am, after all, half Italian.

What a Sunday morning! There I'll be, in my folding chair and slept-in clothes and overnight beard, breaking open a fresh pack of cigarettes—and maybe I'll have a bible in my lap, so when they walk by and ask why I'm not going to church, I can just hold up the bible and they'll forgive me. They have to forgive people with bibles. It's a rule.

Also, I think I'd like to have a goat. Just a small one, mind you, maybe on a leash or something. There's plenty of grass around for the goat to eat. I think goats eat grass. They eat tin cans and glue in cartoons, but this wouldn't be a cartoon goat. This would be a real goat. I wonder if there's a pet shop in the mall. I should ask one of the protestors.

And maybe I'll get another flag to hang somewhere behind me. A big one. I think I would look good sitting in a folding nylon chair behind a giant American flag in the clothes I slept in, and my overnight beard, smoking a cigarette and waving my bible at people while my goat orally trims their lawns.

Also, I'd like to ask the Christians questions. There's really no better way to learn things than to ask questions. I'd ask them things like, "if God rested on the seventh day, and technically Sunday is the end of the work week according to the post-office and really, all of the Western capitalist world, wouldn't this be the seventh day, and won't you be bothering God on his one day off? Surely God must be a capitalist; I won't hear you slandering God with your awful communism. Why don't you go on a Saturday or something? Most people are off on Saturdays, standing in roped-off lines. But God isn't off. Shouldn't we only bother God during the work week? Oh, maybe we could do it on Friday, over lunch hour! We could all get together and have a nice Cobb salad with God on casual Fridays. I'll bet he'd just love my piano tie!"

I wonder about other things. Like, do people ever have sexual thoughts about Jesus? He was pretty tall, I think. And it's well-established that Jesus had a pretty ripped stomach. Just look at all those paintings! I might even ask one of the Christians if it's alright to have sexual thoughts about Jesus. I mean, who better to have sexual thoughts about, right? The man *was* the son of God!

Tomorrow morning, I'm going to get up early and make myself some eggs and toast, and then I'm going to sit outside and greet all those solemn, silly church goers—who are really only bothering God on his only day off—and I'm going to smoke cigarettes and wave the bible in front of Old Glory with my goat and my overnight beard and slept-in clothes, and I'm going to ask everyone why no one jerks off to Jesus. Because I think God would like it better if we all just stayed home on Sundays and left Him alone, but maybe had a good jerk while thinking about His son. I think he'd like that.

They'll probably ask me if I'm gay, but I'm not. Maybe I'll just tell them I'd ask Sophia to feel herself up while thinking of Jesus while the goat and I watch. I think God would have wanted it that way when he wrote the bible in the first place.

. . . .

Volume is often used as a defense mechanism.

Most of the time I'm really not so bitter about this world, but all these rampant gender games, confused politics and religious dogmatism tend to get under my too-thin skin. That, and a steady week living off the road in the middle of nowhere, lying on the hard cold ground, jerking off to ghosts and drinking myself unconscious, may have rendered my brain a tad unstable.

I'm staring at my face in the mirror. Sometimes I want to peel all the skin off, and crawl out of my body altogether. I wonder if this is normal. I wonder if anything can ever be normal, ever, again. I wonder if the things I've seen and done and traversed can ever be normalized, or settled into some nice, quiet and relatively ordinary status quo of satisfaction. I wonder if there's a cold medicine for madness. I wonder what would happen if I drank enough cough syrup?

Sophia hates me. Sophia hates me with the virile dedication of a sexually confused vegan valedictorian law student. She hates me in her straight, pretty, pressed clothes and nice shoes. I've forgotten how or why we ever got on in the first place. I wonder if I'm the last person she knows?

During the day, I do the same thing over and over until I wear a track into the sidewalk. I wake up, I shower, I walk a few miles, I sit in the bookstore, I see a movie, I have a sandwich and two beers, and I walk back.

It all feels so fucking desperate. If I lash out—I lash out the way a starving disregarded dog lashes out in bleak back alleyways. Still, I have this damnable human conscious tugging at me to be something better than a dog. Still, I have this damnable mirror staring back at me, wondering how swollen eyes can talk so very loud.

A week later, Sophia drives me to LAX airport.

. . . .

I am tired. I wander through the bright terminal, tired.

A TSA agent grabs my arm and orders me take off my shoes. He shoots glowing blue light from a small plastic wand inside their very soles.

"Sir—do you hide anything in your shoes?"

"Socks? My ex-wives…"

My things are searched.

31

Two hours later, I get on the plane after a long stop at the airport bar. My eyes, heavier than airplanes, unpropelled, sink to the ground.

. . . .

III. Where is My Mind?

When I finally get back to Alton, I shrug off any notion of jet lag and move immediately into a small house on the outskirts of town, along with a few old and relatively warm-blooded friends.

Henry, once a semi-professional sophist, is now a thinly-spread and rapidly balding stress insurgent enrolled in post-graduate studies at a local college. He is also a part-time dental assistant, horticulturalist, construction worker, baseball card addict, amateur beard farmer, and is the perennial father figure to nearly everyone in town under thirty. He greets me at the door with the slightest hint of eyelids, wearing a beat-up old pair of blue jeans that hang loose despite his husky frame, and the same green Grateful Dead shirt he's been wearing since I met him a hundred fifty three years ago.

"Charlie! Welcome home, brother. Come on in!" he beams.

"Henry. That's really a lovely scent you're wearing. What's it called?"

"Sweat, cheap beer, and baseball cards. It's French, I think. Do you really like it?"

"Oh, it's lovely. You'll have to tear me a page out of the magazine some time."

James Watson is sitting in the same hole in the center of the same couch that he's been occupying for as long as I've known him. By day he is a graphic artist, and by night he is less noble, but equally unqualified. During days off, he visits the video game section of the local Blockbuster with such great frequency that they have renamed it in his honor.

The town, Alton, is now threatening to become something beyond the mere specter of a city it once was—now injected with large chain electronics stores, brand name restaurants, over-priced coffee shops, designer furniture warehouses, plush air-conditioned sixteen screen luxury stadium seated movie theaters, and fashionably empty martini bars.

But the people have remained the same. The mood has remained the same, even if the dress code has gone semi-casual. At least that's still true in my small circle of friends.

I think it's good to be back. I think I'm relieved. When you're away from any place for long enough, you start to the miss mundane comfort of everyday absolute boring certainty. If this is the best the welcoming committee can do, I will happily take it.

. . . .

My neighbor drives a white car.

The inside of her house is a post-tornado collage of clothes, food wrappers, beer cans, cigarettes, and dishes covered with mold older than I am. She is twenty, and she is terribly lovely.

Also, I have the secret suspicion that she may be pure evil.

A spiral-bound manuscript copy of my second novel, that I had made for more money than I care to remember, sits on a shelf in her living room like the farthest, smallest, coldest star in space.

Late at night she tells me she wants to be a muse, and tosses her hair and blinks in earnest like she's trying to tear Odysseus from his roped position at the mast. She has a lazy, easy loveliness about her. It might just be the baseball cards, or the lighting, but in the twilight of the room, every mundane idiotic thing she says is absolutely captivating. You trust her deep brown eyes like you would trust a dog's eyes. You watch her lips part with child-like glee, and count the microscopic beads of sweat on the nape of her perfect swan-like neck with curious, grave envy.

Sometimes I listen to her. When we are alone, she likes to talk about the painful stereotypes surrounding small towns, and all her wild ambition to be something large that contains multitudes. When we are not, she talks about how "fucked up" or "wasted" she, or someone in her company, was the previous night. She talks about the former with delicate care, and the latter with loud optimism like someone watching a football game; like she's trying to keep score. She tells me how determined she is to lead the league in liver damage, lung cancer, and brain cell extinction.

"We call that the triple crown," I tell her.

She goes on, and I am senselessly captivated.

Timothy Lloyd walks in the room, opens a fresh pack of baseball cards, nods, and leaves for work.

The White Car stretches out to reveal her midsection. I can tell, because my eyes have corners. I imagine watching this exquisite display is the modern day twenty-something equivalent of watching Moses part the Red Sea.

. . . .

Eve Saul knocks gingerly on the back door. I immediately know it's her, because I've had ten years to learn that knock. I know her stealthy, steady silent rhythm. I know she will wait for at least ten minutes before bothering to knock again, in case someone is sleeping, or about to achieve inner peace. I know her neck is craned ever-so-slightly to the left, and that she is peering through a small pane of glass into the darkness of the laundry room. I can see the splintering silver-blue light coming off her eyes, and I'd make a two-to-one bet she is either humming or singing quietly to herself. I know a lot of things about her, and she probably knows even more about me. I know that she is anything but evil.

Eve comes in, as always, with a ridiculously bright grin that I am convinced was constructed solely for my benefit, and sits on a small couch in my room.

She is telling me about work. She is telling me that she cannot believe people do things and participate in whatever ordinary imperfect human actions people participate in on a daily basis. Like, the other day someone coughed during a meeting. Imagine! I smile, and glance down at the floor so as not to let on that I too am imperfect and human and ordinary. In ten years, this seems to be the one thing she hasn't figured out about me, or, moreover, about the world—that we are all miserably imperfect. I smile, and I glance down at the floor because I am the king of miserably imperfect.

. . . .

I live indoors.

Tim is attempting to type a paper about a short story he couldn't care less about. The computer trembles under his short, stubby shivering fingers. Henry is taking a shit six feet away. We can hear him singing broken Marvin Gaye songs through the wall. A thin film of brown featherdust drops backwards off the ceiling.

The White Car pulls up next door. Through the window we watch her slinky paper doll figure flutter across the dirt driveway, towards her house, and through the broken screen door which looks like an extra from a Tim Burton movie. For a moment, I am still intrigued enough that I imagine I can actually hear her high, girlish voice raise an extra octave to greet the silky arched back of her cat.

"Man," Tim sighs.

"I know. Yeah..."

"What was I..."

"*The Yellow Wallpaper*. The one where the chick goes crazy. You need a middle paragraph, an educated conclusion, a few sources, a topic sentence, a basic assumption as to theme and then you're practically finished!"

"Right. How do you spell *wallpaper*?"

"The *H* is silent."

Tim sighs and goes back to typing. The computer barks and chews up its own tail.

Through the wall, we hear the shower start and the singing continue. I begin to pace. I am wondering about fast food restaurants.

Chicken or beef? Taco Bell? Pizza? A loaf of bread and a pound of roast beef, ketchup, and a twelve pack of Coke? I wonder if the mail has come yet.

Henry walks out of the bathroom, his misplaced broom hair and ripped Miller High Life t-shirt replaced by a shirt and tie. I'm a little disappointed, and I tell him as much.

We fix Tim's margins, and center the title over his topic sentence. I wonder if I should listen to music?

. . . .

I had thoughts once. I'm laughing at the dead prospect of ghost thoughts.

I like the sound the ceiling fan makes, even though it keeps me awake at night. To me, it sounds like progress. Something in my room is spinning forward, clockwise.

I'm happy with the temperature today. That is something. I walk outside and stare straight up as if to thank the clouds. I look next door to see The White Car that spills slinky things that flutter and dissipate.

Inside, on the counter, beer footprints and unwrapped phantom cheeseburger castles play hopscotch with flies.

"Someone should really take that shit out," The ceiling fan whirs.

"Fuck off."

"What's up, man?"

A leper and a little dog appear. "Nothing. Nothing. Nothing."

I wonder if I'm getting enough sleep? I'm wondering if there's enough iron in my diet. I wonder if listening to the rhythm of your own heartbeat is detrimental to its progress.

The walls at the head of my bed are cool and hypnotizing. I pick at pillows, and pull at dreams even though my eyelids are painted sun-green.

There're a thousand things I should do. Talk to people. Go places. Eat. Shit. Sing. Woody Allen once said, "eighty percent of life is just showing up." I think he said "eighty." I don't care. I could kick Woody Allen's ass.

Sometimes the phone rings. Sometimes someone answers it. Sometimes it rings for days.

I should really clean my room. License plates and oil crayons and wrapping paper, two months late, cover what used to be carpet. Socks and tissues, unrelated, guard the doors and windows. CDs and empty popcorn bags cascade off the shelves. For a moment, I think about diving into the middle of the whole mess, waving my arms back and forth, and calling it a "slacker angel."

Instead, I watch the deleted scenes from "Lost in Translation."

. . . .

Are midgets funny?

Tim is complaining about midgets not being funny. He doesn't like things that make him uncomfortable, like midgets, centennial porn, the word *cul-de-sac*, or most forms of basic human interaction.

"What time is it?"

"Uh—six o'clock?"

"Hmm. What day?"

It's Tuesday. In grade schools, they taught us colors that represented different days of the week. Blue days are for music class. Yellow days are P.E.

The television is debating the political future of refugee mannequin orangutans. We're debating a fifth pack of baseball cards. I'm debating the merits of the bottle of whiskey in my jacket pocket.

Tim is fidgeting. Tim is very good at fidgeting. Besides this, he has an astonishing center of gravity which he often uses to topple those taller than him, which is to say, everyone. Tim's eyes are steady and doglike in an unflinchingly friendly way. You want to trust him when he mumbles desperation. You know that if you're ever in trouble you have a friend who would gladly lay down in traffic if it would make the world right again.

Tim wants to hit up a bar. I'd like to find my legs. Henry wants to follow the yellow brick road and sing about the more off-beat uses of maple syrup.

The phone rings and no one answers it.

. . . .

Sometimes things come in the mail. I put on my least conspicuous hat and walk gingerly by the ghost-white car across the street to check the box. Dead people get more mail than I do. I'm contemplating faking my own death to see if they'll posthumously award me a Sears Catalogue.

Cars purr by along the long, open street and forget to wave. I keep my head down, because I've seen too many old movies.

Back inside, everything smells like burnt doll hair. I run my hand through my own closely-clipped mop, and rub the tops of my eyelids clean off.

During the day, everyone is either asleep or working. I pace the thirty yard track to the bathroom to do my daily reading.

I like the wallpaper in the bathroom. It would smell like the ocean if we ever mopped the floors, or cleaned the counters, or vacuumed, or pulled the mountain of dead soapy hair out of the drain. Sometimes I check the fridge. Still there. The phone rings, and I take off my shoes.

. . . .

I drink another Coke and lick my teeth. Still there.

. . . .

Little strips of paper remind me to do things: Call the car insurance company and tell them that existence precedes essence. Send that girl who works at the Virgin Megastore in Times Square the DVD of that music video you shot last summer. Finish formatting the margins of that short story about unironically charming Satanist midwifes. Find a more efficient path to clean socks.

When the lights click off outside, I pull the little beaded brass rope hanging from my heroic ceiling fan and make everything red. I wonder if the cars passing by think I'm running a brothel? I don't think I could really run a brothel. I'd probably give idealistic lectures to the whores and patrons.

"Just buy her dinner..."

"Just let him buy you dinner..."

. . . .

I get an email from a girl I've never met. She tells me she's contemplating regicide, and I advise her to take up spinning. I send another email to a girl I knew in high school who never had fingers. I call a girl I'll never sleep with. The White Car in the driveway next door disappears. Somewhere, a girl I'll never see again is laughing at me.

"That fucker."

I tell people it doesn't faze me anymore.

"Ahh, I've given up. It's not worth the sweaters."

They nod their heads solemnly, as if I've just said something sage-like.

I'm addicted to my computer. It tells me who's on first, when the second sequel to the movie adaptation of the third extra's character in Lars Von Trier's fourth film is coming out, and what I should think about the latest record by a British band that sounds a little like Radiohead, but sadly, isn't. The display screen tilts backward and imagines pebble rings in childhood swimming holes.

. . . .

The house sounds like rain at night. Things creak and cascade and scurry. I imagine it's just mice, but I hold out the hope that it's secretly the shallow footsteps of quasi-reformed prostitutes skulking around in Sonic Youth t-shirts.

When I open my eyes again, red is yellow.

Every morning still has shades of Christmas. Everything is possible. I lay perfectly still for a while and listen for hoof prints.

Realizing one can't *listen* for hoof prints, I make a motion for the remote.

Bombs! Death! Injury! Panic! Bus rides! Thirty-five degrees and partly cloudy!

Click.

Start getting real.

Click.
No he dihint!
Click.
Hold it. There's a kid out there. Tommy! Get out of there!
Click.
Well, it's a long story, but...
Click.
I'll do it. Whatever it is, I'll do it. I don't care. Whatever it...
Click.
Here's one of California's finest.
Click.
Only the best for...
Click.
Bombs! Death! Injury! Panic! Bus rides

. . . .

Sometimes I actually have dreams, and the buffet gets weird. The food isn't who it's supposed to be. Sometimes I wipe all the cobwebs off of heaven, and it's suddenly morning.

I spend most of the day cleaning and shopping—stocking up on foods that might be deemed nourishing or beneficial, cooking a grand meal, and teaching a few beer cans how to disappear completely.

Today I replace the oppressive red lights in my ceiling with pale blue. It's a banner day, really. I wonder if I remember how to write a proper press release. I think the key is **VERY BOLD TYPE**, and a great deal of exclamation points.

Later, I give up and run through the woods with Henry's dog.

Later still, I wander through a video store with Graham and Tim. We dive like cartoon superheroes through rows of subpar silver screen ejaculations until we find the perfect mix of pretentious art house fodder and achingly modern quasi-cult horror movies.

Feeling half-drugged, and resembling one of the middle characters in the evolution chart, I lead the division towards a tall, beautiful, nymph-like waif, slightly imperfect in completely acceptable places, standing behind the cash register.

"I loooove this movie," she purrs, holding up the case of the achingly modern quasi-cult horror movie choice.

"Me too! Do you want to come over last for blue-lit red wine and discussions of infinite comma-less sentences about indefinable things and accidentally kiss and fall through the ceiling fan with me?"

"Sir?"

"I wonder if you could fit inside one of my shoes? You have such pretty elbows."

"Sir?"

Tim coughs, and nudges me on the arm.

"Hi," I manage, sheepishly. "Hello."

"Are you okay? I said, that'll be $12.51."

In the parking lot, we pass a red Honda civic with a Fugazi bumper sticker as it pulls up six spaces to our left. Lola Thomas—who I'd just had a beautifully unrealistic dream about two nights ago—who I almost wrote or called or telepathed—steps out, and trots alone on past us into the video store. I, barely in my car, honk the horn, wave and evaporate.

All these dead things keep walking over my most famously-irrepressible errors. I suddenly wish I'd never invented street signs.

Back at the house, we throw on the first movie as Graham invents a fog machine and Tim stencils himself into the back wall. Ten minutes later, just as vampires are discovering hollow-tipped bullets, a girl walks in on Morticia Adams tentacles and informs us that her and The White Car, next door, aren't doing anything and wonders if we'll relocate and watch the rest of the movie with them.

Graham and I skip rope across the nascent, dewy backyard. Tim goes home.

I sit next to Morticia Adams, who is quite lovely, and is an unironic Strokes fan.

"What does that have anything to do with…"

"Fuckoff."

"Who are you walking to?"

"Talking."

"You know what I mean."

Morticia Adams blinks.

"Are you all right Charlie?"

"Yeah. Great!"

The White Car pulls a out a limited edition box of baseball cards from underneath the couch, and spreads the wealth. I help her tear the foil apart, and the screen door suddenly becomes flooded with migrant butterflies.

I follow suit, and fall backwards into the nearest shadow of lamplight. My wings twitch, but don't flutter. I try to look like the perfect art-core mutilation of every bad movie paradox in the history of cinema. I steal Johnny Depp's jawbone, and scowl beautifully. I am Bill Murray's halfsmirk. I am Jude Law's eyes, and Harrison Ford's posture. Does anyone notice? I swear I'll turn this car around right now. I'll do it.

I am melting into the wall, and everyone knows it.

I watch the credits roll and go home invisibly to eat tacos with my record collection.

The vapor and seesaw movement of the ground glide through the nothingness of atoms, and the nothingness of humanity, and the nothingness of vapor thoughts hummed at drunken electronic sparrows. At my best moments I run into the most walls, where pure feeling equals existing, and essence is only a mirror image of the accidents we arrange our lives over.

. . . .

I have a dream that Kirsten Dunst and I are sitting on top of the world making beautiful radioactive children. They all come out electric blue. Her eyes and my eyes are so iridescent and immediately striking, that people have instant epileptic fits. All our enemies try to outlaw the colors we create—solid colors so pure—so wildly serene—we even make a black that gives out instant orgasms.

When I wake up, I am the fish with the bicycle again.

Now I'm just tired—too tired to have an actual "mood."

The other day I tried to tell a girl that liver damage is always the fastest way to a man's heart. My most redeeming qualities are often the ones most responsible for my utter ineptitude as a human being.

I'm bored with picnic tables. I suppose things just move in slow motion sometimes. Sometimes they stop.

All the places I've been—seen—all the history, it all means so very little to me now. The best things always happen like weatherman mistakes and cancel the world.

Being in Paris four years ago was awful with just one set of eyes, not to mention all the bread was stale. But coming back—falling asleep in the smallest room on earth with a lone, kind, warm blooded girl with soft nebular skin just killed off every river, palace, painting, or ballet broadcast outdoors over a hundred yards of brick. I have become obsessed by these dead memories. They're my own slow-motion black and white film flashbacks, and I am the worst, most unshaven, pathetic Humphrey Bogart characature in the history of cinema.

It never felt right traveling—seeing all that beauty—alone. I am much too small for all that. I can't keep it all in. It's better here, in the twilight of an empty room. It's easier to make sound where there is no sound. It's easier to hear yourself disappearing when there is nothing to cover up the silence.

I'd rather be an unwritten encyclopedia entry. I'd rather stare at the back of someone's head than at a castle. I'd rather be downwind from a shampoo commercial. I'd rather be a child than a dragon.

It occurs to me that I'm both terrified of and in love with everything. I'm like a blood whore for a gang of emotional vampires. I'm romantically vitriolic. I dive, headfirst, and at light speed into piles of sand hoping I'll make something other than glass. I'm a bag of rocks waiting to be fireworks in city

47

street puddles. I'm the sound of abject patience painting the ground clear.

All I ever wanted to be was smiling light bulb wire.

. . . .

I wake up the next morning, and I write a goodnight letter to the queen of the Martian sandbox.

Later, someone's car takes me to a hardware store. I trade my legs for manic indifference and glue traps.

At home, the phone wanders around, holding up old pictures and laughing. Other than that, the planet is quiet. A little dog lay at my side licking my hands. Its breath smells like a three day showerless summer. Its eyes flutter and grasp.

Sometimes it falls asleep, and starts chirping at the wind and running in place.

. . . .

If someone asked me what I wanted these days, I wonder if I'd be able to answer without raining sarcasm? I wonder if I could fold up until I became light enough to fly? I wonder if my skin could grow through the wallpaper if I left it lying there long enough.

Graham walks through the door and knocks.

"Asshole!"

"Hey! Charlie!"

"Come on in. There's a chair and an ice cube tray."

He takes the latter. His eyes spin silvery webs across his brain, and crawl straight out. It's a safe bet that Graham has stopped taking unleaded. He pulls at his beard as if it was made of Velcro, and he could yank it off and trade it in for an out of print Nation of Ulysses record. He has eyes tattooed on his arms, and I've never before asked him why.

"Graham?"

"Cough."

"Right."

We go to the post office, where they keep all the eyes that crawl out. I have to mail out another fifty three query letters. I am collecting rejections, but the letters don't say that. Not specifically, at least.

The girl in front of us is about our age, but she appears to be about three zeros more comfortable. Her hair is tied up in court, and her slender black skirt smells exactly like her beach house.

An old man behind us makes bitter old man jokes. Graham's skin cracks, and flakes off on the floor.
Then everyone becomes featureless—first red and swollen—then pale to the point of translucence. Graham crawls on the ceiling and hides.

"Hey, that's cheating."

"Can I help the next person?"

"Help! Help!"

. . . .

Ordinary imperfect people do things like get up in the morning and go to work. This is where I part with ordinary imperfect people.

The phone rings.

"Charlie?"

49

"Most of the time, yes."

"Hey man, it's Rawlings. Hey, are you *straight*."

"Is that a personal question, because they told me I'm not supposed to answer…"

"Hey, you know what I mean, right?"

"Yeah. I'm *straight*."

"Cool. Cool. Hey, d'ya mind if I stop by?"

"I'll be here."

Rawlings stops by. Rawlings is a middle-aged, bald, slouching former guitar player with a beer gut that would make Jim Belushi blush. He walks into the house and informs me that, "Mexicans are the new niggers."

"That'll be a hundred dollars." I hand him a small box and attempt to ignore his vast powers over the English language.

"I'm telling you Charlie, they are! Mexicans are the new *niggers*…"

"Here you go."

I wonder if he even imagines words mean things? If you smack an illiterate with a book, does it make a sound?

What is considered as offensive in the world anymore? Preteen homosexuality is a playful adjective, and necrophilia is a televised sporting event. Not that I'm even attempting to compare the two. I mean, ESPN only has so many channels.

I want to tell him to go to hell. I want to tell him to shut his fucking mouth and to get the hell out of my house, and that I'm fucking tired of the assumed racist sexist bullshit that goes along with small towns, and I'm tired of the ease and nonchalant manner at which people slip in and out of stereotypes, and that I'm tired of letting things go. I want to crush his shiny hairless fucking skull with the back of the chair sitting by my desk. I want my resentment of the south to be every bit as magically delicious as his southern resentment.

I picture myself doing this. I see things happening in slow motion. I drift off into them. Rawlings is talking about something, but I'm just smiling. I'm just smiling because his shiny fucking skull is shattered into neat little flakes that hang in the air like paper in a gelatin wind.

I want to do things, but I don't.

"Thanks for supporting the arts." I tell him.

"You bet. Thank you, sir. See ya, Charlie."

. . . .

I put up with a lot of things. One of the things I don't put up with is getting up in the morning and going to work. I tried that once. Actually, to be fair, I tried that over a dozen times. I was a busboy once, a dishwasher twice, a waiter, sales clerk, substitute teacher, go-cart track attendant, house painter, dog walker, second assistant administrative secretary to the interior vice president of the executive subcommittee for explorative inquiries on temporary joint ventures, and a professional college dropout. I used to sell hotdogs at Yankee games in the 1920's. One time, I even got the idea to run across the country, take up table tennis, grow a mustache, and open up a chain of world-famous shrimp restaurants.

Sometimes I just got bored. Sometimes I just got fired. Sometimes, something was happening in another part of the world that just required my immediate, absolute and full attention. Sometimes,

51

what I was doing was making all the hair on the back of my neck freeze into decorative little icicles. Sometimes something starting happening to my vision, like God was taking the 3-D glasses off too quickly. Sometimes the sound of my own heartbeat just got too loud to bear.

But freedom—freedom is a happy baseball card. Pardon the pun.

I like having the freedom to sleep in. I like having the freedom to stay up until the ugly naked vampire hours of the night. I like having the freedom to report these things. I like the slow hovering flakes of madness that swim through freedom's naked eye.

I am a part of that freedom.

. . . .

Everything seems a little off since I got back from California. It's as if every atom in the world has shifted the slightest bit to the right, and someone forgot to send me the memo. My shoes don't quite fit anymore, and I've completely forgotten when I'm supposed to yell, "Yahtzee!"

Everyone is standing in a different place, and we've run out of chairs.

Eve and I used to be inseparable. She had all the time in the world to drive down back roads, just the two of us and her camera, stopping at the hair-curve edge of a ditch to shoot off rolls of black and white film that made even the most desolate corners of town seem cinematic. She used to have this knack for making simplicity seem so complex, so much more vivid and heavy and rich than a first glance could ever give you. She made everything seem so easily beautiful.

I don't remember the last time she even took a picture, or drove down an unnamed road without stopping for directions. Not with me in the car anyway.

Last year, Eve bought a nice little house just outside of town. It is, in fact, quite immaculate. All the colors are perfectly complimentary, and the carpet is so clean you expect to have to take your shoes off and sit on grandma's stiff plastic couch. When I go over there, I feel like I should be sitting at the kiddie table.

She manages one of the new monolith chain stores that have taken over the recently revamped north end of town, wears monochrome poly fibers, and has immaculate posture and braces. When the cocoon finally falls off, I sometimes fear she may end up more June Cleaver with a 401K than June Carter Cash with a camera. She hasn't the time for much art these days. She hardly has any time for me. And I'm a bastard for thinking such things, but I miss my goddamned friend.

Henry, meanwhile, is constantly caught in the crisis of balancing his master's degree with his job, girlfriend, and cologne addiction. He still breaks glasses in bars, still falls over things, and still delivers bastardized late night Buddhist soapbox sermons with the best of them—but he is slipping. The development of his mind is lagging slightly behind the rate of growth of his stomach, and his ambition for greatness is lagging well behind the reality of the work he must do to get there, which is, by all views, killing him.

Tim, who seemed absolutely doomed altogether just two years ago, has managed to balance his old life with all the systems which daily seem about to do his life in. He still has the same job, the same six friends, the same disposition of negativism, the same baseball card habits, the same roadblock on dreams, the same intolerance for systems, and the same befuddlement and ache in the great demonic coat hanger world of romance. He is the healthy one.

Others are simply gone altogether. No contract negotiations, no soap opera coma, just gone.

I feel like the last of a sort of dinosaur. I wonder if I'll ever end up in a museum? I wonder if I'll ever become warm-blooded again?

Sometimes I prick myself on the back of the neck with the sharp end of a tack. I like to pretend I can almost feel it, but I wonder if I'll ever feel the full effect of anything anymore. The mirror in my room is so very loud, but I don't feel like dancing.

. . . .

It's still outside. Cars drive by and say things in their hushed wake, but I don't reply.

All the trees in the backyard have arms. They wave back and forth like things resting on water. Only, the trees wave sideways.

It's almost June again, and the grass is turning back from the dim egg-yolk yellow it assumed all winter, to scorched tones of green and brown. The yard is covered in little white flowers that seem to be doubling as bee gas stations, or perhaps motels that rent rooms by the hour.

Everything in the summer seems so ephemeral. The sun suddenly decides to be warm again, the ocean starts singing about French fries, and all the clothes just fall off. Somewhere, a barbeque is attracting beerhands. Somewhere, there's a flick of an eyelash that wasn't there in March.

Everything is again becoming a part of that strange honey-scented buzzing. The insects hum on their way to the next great raid. Cars hum towards humming oceans. Crowds hum in naked unison. I, meanwhile, am wondering how to avoid disappearing altogether.

. . . .

At night the house fills up with people, and music that overcompensated for its shortcomings with massive amounts of volume, followed by tables of food, grills, fires that burn sideways and upside-down, centrifugal pacing, two-toned plastic cups and hand pumps, big eyes, bigger looks, hops, corners, lines and factions, and the odd individuals leering at the bastard colors of the setting sun, wondering where to hide, or how to get lost.

Henry leans sideways in the doorway and tells the early crowd an overlong story about the merits of Asian leprosy in a low, garbled voice. He swings a plastic cup in his right hand back and forth in comic illustration, until he is almost completely covered in foam, slaps himself twice on the knee, and begins laughing uncontrollably. His eyes look like paranoid Venetian blinds painted blood-red.

I sit on the porch making sandcastles with the soles of several discarded tennis shoes. I try to tell people I have a tongue. I try to trade eyes—

One pair is tall and thin, and has let all the fair, summer portions of her skin out for air. I don't recognize her; I have no idea who she is, but I still attempt to tell her how lonely my fingers are, and that I have black sheets and write poetry when I'm swimming. I wonder if she speaks telepathic Mid-Atlantic sign language?

"I like things," I tell her loudly. "Do you also like things?"

She opens her mouth and points to the fact that her tongue has already wandered off with someone else.

The crowd splits into several middle school subsections, with most of the women sitting on couches indoors, talking about things that almost happened that one time, but didn't, because people have Facebook accounts. The men huddle up with plastic cup facemasks, talking about things that will never happen, and should we be on Facebook right now? Let's take a picture! Everyone's laughing, and yelling about things they wish were happening. Somewhere, a bell rings.

. . . .

Eventually, the house overflows altogether. The jocks, the heads, the boilers, the steam, the on-girls, the screamers, the background and quiet, the invisibly loud, the hummers, the beardless, the cringed, the caped, the cult, the cool, the collars, the naked, and the famous all gather in the a.m. salad like a giant United Nations after party directed by David Lynch.

By now, the bathtub has been filled and refilled with beer repacked in ice, and my dresser has become kindling for the giant bonfire in the backyard.

I am waiting for something to happen. I have a beer, a shot, a Coke and a water, trying to pace myself. I walk around. I collect DNA. I invent life stories based on shadows cast by blinking eyelashes, and I watch the world slowly start to spin off its axis.

The White Car walks by. I think she's dancing.

"Charlie!" she sings.

"That's the correct answer; now let's see how much you wagered..."

"What are you doing?"

"Uh—I think there's party going on somewhere. I..."

"I know. I see. It's crazy!" She pauses and gleams, "I think I'm going to get

drunker than I've ever been before!" Her face lights up like cartoon Christmas.

"Hey, good for you! So many people your age lack goals these days."

Is drunker a word? I wonder about things. I watch all her parts walk off into the dancing ashes.

I watch the dogs, most of which I've never seen before, run erratic circles in the backyard and fall down. I imagine them starting a trend. I imagine all the bodies we'll have in the morning. I wonder if we have a good shovel?

Eve walks in. No one blinks. I check everyone's pulse.

She tells me about the giant monkey costume she had to wear to work today, and shows me how to do the running man. I consider pouring out my drink and wonder again about that shovel.

We watch the fireworks from a nearby minor league baseball game explode over the treeline in the backyard.

Inside, a girl I used to know asks me what I've been doing. I show her the stack of books in my room, and she invites me to vacation with her on Neptune. I take a rain check, because I don't approve of her eyebrows.

The house spills outside, and runs its foamy fingers down the empty street. I walk into the kitchen. The floors we cleaned a week ago are starting to come apart; the counters are full of floaters and flooded ashtrays.

Everyone's walking around in a strange sort of slow-motion evolutionary science class film run backwards. Or, maybe it's a public service announcement, or the world's most authentic after school special. "This is your walk on baseball cards. This is your haircut after eleven beers. This is the volume of your voice on tequila." I'm waiting for someone to start a fire in the middle of the living room, or invent a picture language on the ceiling.

Eve and I try to make it back outside, but I run into a girl on the way and lose her. She tells me her name is Karen and that we've met before, and I agree to believe her. We look for Eve, but then I lose her too.

I see Graham standing by the fire and notice that all his skin is on, so I leave him to look for the girls, but lose my beer in the process.

Three weeks later, I find Karen hiding behind the sofa next to the remote. She sees me, and flashes the most unironic, beautiful smile I've seen all night. I put an imaginary crown on her head and offer her a beer, but she declines, holding up a bottle of vodka.

"Hey, even better!" I say.

"So, why aren't you drinking?" she asks loudly.

"I'm pacing myself."

"*Awwww*! Don't. Have fun. Get *lost*."

"And miss all this? Someone has to remember this night—for posterity—or at least to fill out the police report in the morning." We might as well be talking over helicopters.

"Oh, come on! You'll be fine. I'll catch you if you fall over. Scout's honor!"

"Yeah?"

"Absolutely."

I am drinking.

We go into the backyard and watch the fire.

"My dresser's in there somewhere," I tell her.

A crowd of people sit in the cab of a large green pickup truck, passing a bottle of whiskey as if it contained the antidote. I can't make out their faces, but then again, neither can they.

The grass in the field behind the fire is almost eye-level. You can almost hear it growing. It slumps over gracefully, and springs back like a rubbery metronome. I consider asking it to dance.

The sky is still; a little cloudy, but frozen that way. The world is grey and brassy-red and flickering. Other than The White Car's Tim Burton set piece, there isn't another house for several hundred yards. If Robert Stack were here, we'd all be abducted by UFOs and forced to grow beards and develop slow, confused southern accents.

I convince Karen to run through the field with me. We chase each other, and make grass waves until one of us recalls the existence of ticks, and decides it might be more fun to go inside and get liver damage.

On the way in, someone slurs something about two inches of standing water in the bathroom. I go in to investigate and find Jude and James in the middle of a WB season finale shouting match in the back hallway. Their faces are dull and red, but their hair gel is impeccable. I jump in between them and ring the bell between rounds. Jude's towering frame heaves quickly, then freezes. I watch as his eyes become three-dimensional. Watson pulls off his glasses and sneers. I stand between them with my arms out like a cross.

Everyone's on the verge of putting on capes, burning off their eyebrows, sharpening their eyes into knives, fixing their war paint, and throwing their medals back over the wall. There's a girl crying in the living room. Someone says something about a stripper and a film crew in the back bedroom. I don't know exactly what's happening, but I think the coffee's ready. "Check, please?"

Everything slows down, pauses, and then speeds back up. I hear the air split, feel something warm against my shoulder, hit someone in the chest, and force a door closed.

"Someone tell me what the fuck is going on!" I yell.

"It's all just a misunderstanding."

"Of what?"

Someone starts screaming in Watson's room. I see Henry in the corner sharpening his eyes, and realize that it's his girl that's been crying.

"She walked in, and someone…"

Henry charges the door. I block him in the narrow hallway, and Jude grabs him from behind. No one moves.

I tell The White Car to take the blue team next door for a pack of baseball cards, then tell the red team they've got five minutes to get the fuck out of my sight.

I look in the bathroom. There really are two inches of standing water. The ice has finally melted.

Someone punches a hole through the wall behind me. The fist, stuck, struggling through plaster, is the only discernible sound for miles. Ashes.

Graham catches me at the other end of the house, and holds out a shiny new pack of baseball cards sympathetically. I nod, and Karen and I follow him into my room.

"For christsakes, turn the music up." Ashes, ashes.

Graham leaves an hour later. Karen stays. "What happened earlier? All that shouting and something about needing a ferry to go to the bathroom?" she asks innocently.

"Oh, we call that *Tuesday*."

Karen laughs with her mouth open. My eyes focus in on the gleaming silver light living under her tongue, and I feel my head float off slowly and to the right.

We turn off lights, chase the breath out of each other, and disappear into the blacksheets.

. . . .

In the morning, the sheets are gone. I trace the outline of the body next to me and wonder why we ever invented sheets.

When my fingers hit the small of her back, she sighs a little and falls back deeper into sleep. There's some kind of indiscernible shape carved there. I trace the blue outline past St. Charles Place, and take a ride on the Reading.

There's an overturned ashtray in the middle of the room. There're a few beer cans, and a small village of matchsticks. I stare at the jagged red triangles of a painting I murdered that hangs just to the left of the bed. I wonder what they mean?

I tiptoe out, through the kitchen, and into the newly aquatic bathroom. The house smells like a giant wet ashtray. I give up.

Later, we watch a movie until it freezes midway and turns black. I kiss Karen apologetically. I feel the cool bolt in her tongue and start to get lost again.

Her head spins sideways, then dives. We turn over and I climb inside to chase the breath out. She groans.

I hold her hands down against the sheetless bed. I watch the L-shape of her cheekbone tighten as she pauses and dies, then I climb in further, watching, holding my breath. I kiss her. I move my arms around her little waist. I pull back to see her heavy bottom lip arch into a smile, then gasp, then shut tight. I watch her mouth part and her eyes flicker closed. I zoom in on each shimmering drop of sweat. It's like staring at a new color. I die a little. I want to die more.

We spin around. We move backwards, sideways. We pace the ceiling. We revolve around the room, and pull at each other's limbs until the knot is almost suffocating.

We lay there until nightfall.

. . . .

I see Karen again a few days later. She's standing in the doorway of a third story apartment surrounded by boxes, about to go home for the summer. I like Karen, because she is twenty and tastes like it, and because she's too young to be jaded, and too old to be too easily offended. I like Karen because she makes me feel a little less apocalyptic.

We climb down the stairs together, across the parking lot to a friend's apartment. Inside, there are two girls knitting and drinking beer, surrounded by boxes. I stare at them, wondering if they can read minds.

"What, you've never seen a girl get fucked up while knitting an afghan?" one quips.

"Nope. And now I have seen everything."

A large black and white dog that ought to have a handkerchief tied around his neck jumps us, and wags its long, confused tail happily.

I have a beer while the girls talk about a hometown I've never been to, and am sure I will never see.

The dog fetches a little green Frankenstein of a tennis ball, and pushes it up into my lap. When I hold it up, its ears perk up, and it dives onto its back in anticipation.

"Hey Karen! Look, she's got your eyes."

Karen jabs an elbow into my side, and shoots me a sweetly embarrassed look.

I have another beer.

Later, back across the parking lot and stairs that seem to've grown taller, Karen and I put on a movie and forget to watch it.

In the morning she kisses me goodbye and tells me she'll call when she comes back in the fall. I nod in agreement, but I know better.

. . . .

Summer in a small college town is a lot like winter in a prospector town after the gold rush dried up. Sometimes we sit on the porch just to see what floats by, but it's never anything more than sand.

Graham walks in and out of the room, playing records one song at a time.

At six o'clock we watch the Simpsons and open another pack of cards.

. . . .

I sit in the passenger seat as Tim and I circle the town, talking about all the indecisions and revisions which a moment will reverse.

"So, Karen went home?"

"Yeah. It was fun, but she had to go back to her home planet eventually."

"Damnit! Why aren't there ever any girls in this town? All we've got is rentals."

"Yeah. And the late fees will kill you."

"I talked to that counter girl again today," Tim says hopefully. "She almost remembered my name. What should I do?"

"Did you have your name tag on?"

"Yeah, but it says *Escobar* or something. I make a new one every day. It passes the time."

"You should go back. Maybe she'd prefer a *Pablo*."

"She looks so good in blue polyester and khaki. How is that possible?"

"It has something to do with Newton's fourth law..."

We drive around for hours. Sometimes we stop somewhere, and I buy a Coke.

. . . .

Eve is sitting on a small couch in my room. We're having a beer, and talking about the startling imperfections of humanity.

A large, rectangular cardboard box blinks at me from across the room, half hidden behind a pile of mail.

"Tell her."

I blink back at it.

"Be quiet, freedom."

"Tell her."

"Tell her what? Go to hell."

"Tee eee elle elle."

"She wouldn't understand."

"What's to understand? This is what you do now. This is *freedom* talking."

I take a sip from the green bottle in my hand, and pretend not to notice myself noticing things; I steer my eyes back, and hope she doesn't trace them.

"Charlie?"

"What? Yeah. Sorry."

"Are you all right? You seem..."

"Nothing. Just—tired. I'm just a little tired. You know me; you know I don't sleep." I run my hand around the swollen fingerprints lining the outside of my throat. I cough a little, hiding the sound in my hands.

"Yeah. I'm pretty tired too," Eve yawns as if she means to convince me. She makes that yawning noise that people make.

. . . .

At the end of the day, there's a lot of confusion, and a strange empty feeling in my stomach unfulfilled by McDonald's fries and a Coke, or dreaming dream girls by the imaginary lake, handing out kingdoms and heart flags when I only bought black socks and poor manners for the perfect blonde rainbows of my dreams, nodding—

"You almost asked me something…"

"No, I didn't."

I wish a lot of things. Sometimes the oven cooks everything evenly, and the world yawns away the hours, and the sun doesn't tan the pages of my books, and all those indefinable things aren't blurred in light. I remember there being more of these things a year ago; two years; ten. I'm at a crossroads. I'm starting to believe things have solidly changed for the liquid. I'm starting to wonder why I never learned to swim.

Are pages falling off the calendar? I don't have any sense of time anymore. Sometimes, I notice the sun disappearing, and I try to put it all into context.

People come and go and leave pictures of Andrew Jackson on top of my desk. In return, I hand them a wrinkled pack of baseball cards, and complete entire conversations in nods and hand gestures.

What happened to legs on the ceiling and tongues in the air? Or strange noises swallowed up and blinking, arms prickly from living under warm flesh all night, toes pointed to the North Star, God's name sung outside of church, Lewis and Clark the nape of your neck?

"Where the hell did you run off to?"

"I threw a penny in the well and wished I hadn't."

. . . .

IV. Nightclubbing.

No one moves in the morning; no one breathes. The house rests on the slim handshake of fog, caressing bad grass haircuts in the backyard.

I lay on my back for seconds, hours or weeks, soaking up the dull, comforting textures of unraveling thread. The television keeps me company, assuring me we've caught another evil doer, made over another bored housewife, and may well in fact be on the road to more perfectly understanding why Barbie is so very, very bad.

Rows of abandoned brown glass bottles become major feats of Chinese architecture, gathering nightly on crumbling windowsills, living in the living room. Henry's dog lays, panting lightly, on its side contemplating an awkward mouthful of grass vomit. No one moves.

Every room in the house has white walls. My white walls house several abstract expressionist paintings, a badly organized section of multicolored push pins and appointments, a photocopy of an extended middle finger, a few popped balloons, several coffee-stained business cards, an old decaying envelope with a Thomas Wolfe stamp, an alarm clock hung upside down for better radio reception, a framed picture of George and Laura Bush caught in the middle of an awkward tango, and a two-foot long wooden mask outfitted with a doo-rag and a crumbling pair of seventies cop glasses.

The yellowing white carpet is all but invisible underneath stacks of French-to-English dictionaries, trumpets, old restaurant carryout boxes with unfinished poem lids, numerous baseball card storage devices, several odd pair of used socks, a large spool of unraveled speaker wire, crumpled napkins, match-head corpses, belt snakes, an innumerous amount of unused phone numbers, eleven hundred books on literary agents arranged Altair-to-Zack, and several other articles of various sad ephemera and prolonged cosmic boredom.

I haven't had a day job in well over a year now. I'm not quite sure how that came to be; I'm often not even sure how I get home at the end of the night, or who exactly is to blame for the decline of western civilization, or the actual definitive reason why the sky isn't exactly blue beyond some simplistic explanation of atmospheric tendencies toward prisms and light filters. But I do like the freedom.

Eve shows up at around 5:30, wearing a new level of eyeliner and a convincingly tight light blue t-shirt with the phrase, "support your local poet" written across the modest protrusion of her breasts.

She comes in, and sits on the corner of my bed.

"So…that's a lot of speaker wire." she says, her right eyebrow hovering high over her head.

"Yeah. I was going to run a direct line to the nearest radio station. The reception here is just awful."

"Do you still want to hit up karaoke night later?"

"Yeah. That sounds good—It'll be like having poor reception with a cash bar."

Watson walks through the open door, cranes his neck through the open doorway, and gives birth to a slow, crooked smile.

"Hey Fehhhhlllllll," he says in a slow, deliberate drawl.

"Watson."

"Can I speak with you in the kitchen for a moment?"

"Sure."

"I don't suppose you've been to the mall lately?"

"The...?"

"The card shop, perhaps?"

"Ah. You haven't been getting enough fiber again, have you?"

"No sir, I have not."

"Right. Well, we'll just have to do something about that then, won't we? Can you distract Eve for a second?"

"Dancing elephants?"

"Make her a drink or something."

"I'm on it."

At 9:30, the three of us pull into the parking lot of a local bar, a little loopy on circus peanuts, and walk inside. A century of organized sports lay like Walt Disney's corpse under a thousand layers of transparent lacquer at each table.

We are seated at the "first fifty years of the NFL" booth, and given my current favorite waitress in the known universe: a short, pretty, lean, and uncommonly kind and shimmering little thing called Gwen. She skips up to us, and takes our drink orders in a deliberately slouched freeze frame pose that makes her resemble some kind of 1950s movie poster. Am I fooled? Completely, happily, and unequivocally.

Watson begins telling Mark Twain-style stories that never begin or end, but drift just enough to hold our attention between deliveries of drinks. When he stumbles too much I change stations, getting lost on all the blurry faces sitting at the bar.

I spot the ex-girlfriend of a coworker's former roommate's previous state of unemployment, whose name I can't quite place. She walks by with a young man with an excellent soccer riot haircut, and I tip my glass and demand they join us.

Eve and Watson shoot me confused dog looks.

"Woof!" I assure them.

"Hahlow," the young man says, sitting down.

"Are you guys getting any food tonight?" Gwen, now highly magnetized, asks.

"Noaw fanks, mate. I fink I'd like to proceed directly untuo tha intrafenous injection ahf haard lickah, please."

"Aye, so yoo throaw it dowen strrr-eight like that then?"

"Aye, I half dun this before."

"Cheers, yeah, I cun seah that."

"You're legit, then aren't you?" I ask sheepishly.

"Yeah, buggah. That'I am."

Gwen shakes her pretty head at me, and brings us another round of beers. I tear the tag from the back of Watson's shirt, fashion a ring, and propose to her as she turns the slightest shade of peach.

Eve and the nameless girl flip through a laminated folder of karaoke options, picking out Blondie, Pat Benatar, Beth Orton, Leona Naess, and Olivia Newton John songs that they'll never have the courage to sing.

Watson and I talk about our little kid pirate fantasies, the imaginary girls laughing at the pink air by the bar, ceiling fans, cigarette death, and the absurd number of seemingly constipated athletes doing back flips on our tabletop. But truthfully, I am lost in electric waitressland. If I had a superpower, it would be the uncanny ability to fall in love with a relative stranger in roughly the time it takes to run the fifty-yard dash—in an F16.

When I close my eyes, Gwen and I are tucked away somewhere watching Fellini films in the soft dusk of her bedroom, spilling out occasionally through cool, late-autumn open-windowed rhyming dictionaries of blissful disconnect from everything not taking place at this exact second in time. When I was eight, I wanted to be a pirate, Batman, or Luke Skywalker. Tonight, I want to be a waitress blanket, and tomorrow I'll wish I were a bead of sweat on the small of her slightly pale, flat stomach.

Watson and I leave at around midnight. I slip Gwen my phone number on the way out, and pretend people are still genuine enough to discharge hope. Something resembling a gratified laugh escapes my lips, and I secretly remind myself not to talk to anyone, anymore. Ever.

. . . .

The next night, Tim and I go out to another local bar to watch the arcade fire of blinking lights and bad music, and all girls that won't sleep with us walking around in next to nothing, or swinging by on imaginary chartreuse carnival horses.

Walking through the front doors is sort of like walking through the gates at Jurassic Park; they both share the same incommodious wooden entrance, and about equal chance of being trampled by feral herds of starved predators.

Inside, we can't help but staring at all the smoke and hot air balloons hanging over the dance floor heartbeat assimilator magnet. We watch, transfixed, as a group of girls in the center of the blender hop on one foot and wave their flippers in the air wildly, racing to juggle the falling bubbles on the bridges of their perfect perky extended noses. Others sway awkwardly in nightclub camouflage and unironic amounts of eyeliner, shouting backwards at screeching snow monsters.

I get a drink at the bar.

Tim is doing his best to jiggle like a retarded piñata over the invisible Teflon coat covering everyone on the dance floor. I'm pretending I'm a hit man chewing hit man gum, which is really only the chapped edges of my swollen bottom lip.

Riverrun past the bathroom, aiding mute sirens to the sure thing of having eyes, unequivocal coughs, smoke signals, purse-lips, button laughs, hair wanderings, wig politicians, elbow prophets, and shouted drink orders swinging from the softest parts of my right ear.

If I turn around too quickly, an entire generation might trip over the guard rails and fall to their horrific death. There's really only one saving grace—one thing which sets us apart—that makes humanity the so far superior state of semi-conscious celestial being.

That's right. I'm talking about Velcro.

Velcro on the stuffed cousins of preternatural killers. Velcro on the shoes you'd never get mugged over. Velcro on our hearts on the morning after. Velcro on the urge to consume. Velcro on the backs of lucky assholes. Velcro on the sex for breathing. Velcro on the time it takes to forget.

Suddenly, down come the paper rain storms, and a dancer strikes a cartoon balloon with a closed fist, sending it high into the upper atmosphere. I watch the DJ looking amazingly unfazed in background of it all while downing my eighteenth sugary rum runner.

And the moon is on the ceiling. And the stars are humming along brightly, overhead.

Walk fifty yards, and you're still inside. Walk fifty more. A hundred, two hundred. Climb out of the tarfloor dance blender, and wander upstairs among the dead and the committed. Follow a few directionless leads just for the view. Imagine there's something besides fake IDs and former high school quarterbacks under her pillow. Imagine skeletons slightly better dressed, but ten thousand times less fragrant. Imagine me not imagining everything. Stare and look down. Follow, duck, retreat and maintain a high state of alert.

Stare at the exposed salty slant of skin strung between her hipbones. Follow the Milky Way to her heart. Talk about the weather—Tell her you're starving for psychic justification, or that lately you've been feeling like you've capsized over an emerald sea of expectation. Ask for a lift to the ceiling. Promise to make her dinner on Saturn next Tuesday.

You might think I must be dancing by now, but you would be wrong. I am nodding my head slightly to the beat, because I am a pirate. I would more than nod my head, but the nerve centers of my brain don't seem to be as well attached as they were when we arrived. And what's this stuck to my shoes? While everyone else urges fame and empathy mirrors, I will remain a secretly clever ten year old in a large empty house with an even larger cape.

I wonder if anyone can see me being a pirate? By another eye, I may appear to be no more than a wooden yard sale Indian. You wouldn't think future president, or the man who beat Jesus Christ at Monopoly. You wouldn't think I had ever stepped in grape jello, or hung up the telephone on the best thighs of my generation. Again, you would be wrong.

Tim is having a mild convulsion in the middle of it all. His face is a burgundy blur. A crowd of people move slightly away, and to the left.

My head falls against my left shoulder.

Oh! They're supposed to be sideways! I get it now.

I wonder if I'm allowed to walk over the sand parts with a drink in my hand? There must be an Italian embassy somewhere behind the waitress stand.

I must be indoors and on Neptune. I may even be late for dinner. I resolve, as just compensation, to buy all remaining invisible girls flowers.

Water is falling into the drains in desperate gushes outside. Some survivors stick around for the slow limbo death of 2 a.m., but Tim suggests we "leave the party before the party leaves us." I acquiesce, and wonder if I can still buy a two-year-old hotdog at a convenience store on the way home.

. . . .

I close my eyes and rub my eyelids. Still there.

. . . .

"Hey, Charlie?" a voice clearly attached to a beard asks.

"Hey, Henry?"

"You got a minute?"

"What's up? Are we playing twenty questions?"

"I was wondering if you could spot me another pack?"

"Wall of shame?"

"Wall of shame."

I add a one and a five next to Henry's name. There are already a good half-dozen ones and fives crossed out on the handmade baseball card dealer spreadsheet hanging over my desk. The White Car and Morticia Adams each have their own ones and fives. Watson and Tim share the number 30. Graham is in for 50. Others go as high as 100. I am thinking of charging interest, or, in the girls' case, asking them to show a little thigh.

I wonder if I could increase my dividends by advertising on television? I could wear a snappy suit, and scream about the rapacity in which I need to make room for new inventory. Are dancing monkeys still considered tasteful?

. . . .

The White Car takes two steps into the bar before her cell starts digging a hole in her back pocket. She rushes off, as if she might be secretly changing into Superman. I watch her disappear like a six-year-old might watch someone leaving a trail of puppies behind. The lazy scraps of clothing she rolls around in at home have been masterfully replaced by a strange green and white-striped fabric that sticks perfectly to the faint contours of her statuesque lower half. Billy Crystal hands me the Academy Award for pretending not to notice.

Marley and I hit up a game of pool while she flies high over Metropolis. He sinks a four off the break, and nails the eight into the far left corner a few shots later.

"Fuck," I deadpan.

"I know, right? It's like I've actually played this game before," he says, smiling enormously.

"Shut up and get us another round of quarters."

"Yes'ah massah! get yo quarters for yo right-way, massah. Sho'ah nuff."

"You calling me a racist?"

"No, I'm calling you a shitty pool player."

"Fair enough."

"So, what are we drinking?"

"Ambivalence."

"Sounds about right. So—what about these girls?"

"When you were a kid, did you ever have any of those capsules that turned into sponge dinosaurs when you added water?"

"Yeah. I Remember those. Sure."

"These girls—they're just the opposite."

I look around under my breath while Marley re-racks. Several tables of neat hair gel gangs fill up the empty space between us and the few wandering gazelles who've strayed far enough from the herd.

If the wild plains of Africa looked like this, one might expect a documentary on vegan packs of lions. We out-number our prospective entrees at least three-to-one, and are already well behind in the interspecies conspiracy of smirks going on around us. Only a pair of old black pool sharks coolly nursing cigarettes, and deconstructing the air at a corner table seem destined for any real state of Zen. The thin handful of women at the bar don't look our way, but slowly desiccate back into their thin plastic shells.

An hour later, The White Car reappears with Morticia Adams, who seems to be advertising the availability of her lower half in a painted-on, worn-in jean skirt that frays just below her ankles. I pretend to pretend not to notice, but conspicuously can't help watching the little threads of denim dancing on her toes a little dreamily.

The White Car says something which is presumably in another language, and Marley and I manage to nod our heads as they slither by.

Even the girls we know don't want to be seen with us. Marley is tall and fit enough to match anyone in the bar, but his wit is a little too coarse, and I'm still dressed a little too-much like a hit man on a nervous day off; the underside of my bottom lip rips open and turns my invisible necktie bright scarlet.

Fresh tubes of hair gel walk in and rob jazz entrances. Each one of them knows our girls, and each one stops by and invites them to impossible parties in other solar systems. By rough estimate, there are approximately 248 impossibly essential gatherings occurring tonight in this galaxy alone.

Cigarette smoke filters in and out of the collective lungs of the room. We all share that—and not much else.

The White Stripes come on over the house stereo, but are not turned up. Doors swing open. Shaking hands are shook. Eyebrows are pierced, and leather shoes are polished, and pool cues are retrieved from lock boxes. Waitresses wear circular paths around the bar. Campy color photos of local cover bands hang over the bathroom stalls. A lone thirty-year-old winds up and hammers his sweaty swollen palm over the faded yellow trackball of an arcade game.

Girls at the bar play Linda Blair neck games. Boys at pool tables wander off and disappear. Things ring, chirp, and shimmer vacantly.

I leave a little before 1 a.m. to hit another bar down the street, where I happily find Henry shattering oversized glasses of beers against a hard tile floor. We kill the last good hour of the night mopping the world up with our feet and pretending to look the other way.

. . . .

The world is dead. The world is golden and crisp, like death. The blue lamplight in my room is both dawn-light and death-light; wakelike. On the far side of the left wall, I've tacked rejection letters from some of the most prominent publishers and agents in the world. I am staring at them, somehow a little proud. Somewhere underneath it all is one gleaming declaration of acceptance.

The world has the texture of old letters. There are certain things—certain moments preserved in this room—but they too are growing slowly brown, like old paper.

My skin feels like old paper. My eyes have been stamped New York, Washington, Paris, Vienna, Florence. My heart has been stamped Audrey, Cassandra, Joan, Grace, Lola.

Bottles of wine sit, half-drunk on the desk, turning back into grapes. The reds taste like the last spark of autumn or bitter slow jazz melodies, and the whites taste like tin cans and ash, or the promise of new snow.

I want to move again, but I'm out of stamps. I want to fall for something again, but all the women in my life are fast becoming the same—blurring into the same unrecognizable soup. The best are in love with me, but won't touch me. The worst won't put my body down, but can't pick up my mind. I wake up, talk to the latter, and try to go to bed with the former.

If only I could combine everything; If only the cut and paste commands on my computer worked just as well in my life. If only I could yell "tech support" in a crowded bar. These things are tacked on the walls of my brain. Sometimes I am a little proud of rejection, invisibility, and my nervous hit man attire. Sometimes I wish I were dying a little more. All these things—

Human. Humanity. Impurity. Hope. Texture. Time. A world without gravity. A graveyard in the afternoon. A honeymoon morning. A newborn nightlife; if only I could find something alive to match the dull, golden glow of the dusk light in this room, at this very moment.

. . . .

It's been raining for twelve hours now. At one point, the rain swapped species and froze to the windows. Then it swayed down slowly. Then it melted into nothing.

The wind is running linebacker rushes into the walls. Every now and then, the foundation shivers and swings back and forth like an overburdened pendulum. I stare at the mathematical verve of the architecture, unfazed. I wish I had something else to stare at. I wish all this flat precision were erased. I'm game for circular imprudence.

All day long the phone rings for no one.

"Switch your long distance plan!"

"Accept our free giveaway trip to the island of misfit toys!"

"Try our product free for thirty days, and solve all your worldly problems in fifteen minutes or less!!!"

I stand by the answering machine with a handful of rotten fruit, pausing only enough to shave my eyebrows clean off into the bare sink.

I do lots of things; I leap couches in a single bound; I clear the table; I read Spin magazine cover-to-cover; I figure out the alternate version of a song I've never heard on Henry's old guitar; I shave off all the remaining facial hair my electric razor can handle.

I shower, and patronize a liquor store where I'm told to "drink lots" and "stay dry." I nod, and suppose the two might possibly go together. I wonder if I need glasses, and squint a little at stop signs. I park. I open doors and catch an earful of ice. I run around outside wearing nothing but my socks. I write letters to people I'll never meet.

I make a phone call. The voice at the other end tells me it has no plans tomorrow.

I grab a handful of individually packaged cranberry juice boxes, add them to a bottle of vodka and a tray of ice, and begin to say goodbye to light and earthlegs.

. . . .

In the morning, I drive to the city. I pass by an off ramp that used to get me off for the price of a hotel room. I pass by the streets I used to circle while a girl peeked into her parents' bedroom to make the sure the coast was clear. I pass by her house, and my lungs instinctively fill up with imaginary cigarette smoke.

Things taste different across the bridge; things taste like first-time things, like the dead skin from someone else's lips, or the taste of six kinds of hard liquor poured together into a small bottle of mouthwash.

Clare Sini is walking backwards up the stone steps to her door. I am following her deep into the rabbit hole. I am taking the blue pill.

The first time I met her, I fell in love with her immediately. I don't even remember how I met her, or where, or why; she's one of those people who exist permanently on the outskirts of reality; one of those people you see twice a decade but live for every day. She's the kind of alien concept you dream about when the culmination of your memory washes everything together into an odd, dreamy blur of nostalgic perfection; you don't ever expect to be with someone like her. because people like her don't really exist—you watch them in movie theaters, and you read about them in award-winning novels, but no one ever actually gets to take them out to dinner, or wrap them up in your pillow case and expect them to be there in the morning.

This is not to say she is perfect. Rather, this is to say she is off in all the best ways possible; she's an artist with no identifiable medium—a chronic screamer at streetlights—and she posseses a liver the size of an average British rock star. But she's also oddly gentle underneath all that manic fury and foggy magic.

You get the impression that if you caught her on just the right day, she might end up curled and purring, laying next to you, explaining exactly how one makes thirty minute brownies in twenty minutes. You wonder if this odd combination of Basquiat, Florence Henderson, and Curly from the Three Stooges is even possible, or if you're simply slipping into some overly medicated alternate universe.

You stare hypnotized at her too-blue prism eyes and slow ungraceful gigantic bottom lip that droops like a frail tree limb after an ice storm, and forget to wonder, or to care or if you are imagining any or all of this.

Claire currently has one of the more unfortunate boyfriends on the planet, and is currently telling me all about him. I don't suppose he is real either.

"What's that look for?" she asks, scrunching her face and twisting her features into even more cartoonish perfection.

"Ah Claire—next to you, I'm a blind kitten."

She laughs at this. We're pretending we're old friends who know each other's gestures and gibes all too blindly. The blue pill has kicked in, and all the impossible questions and tight-rope balances between what is real and what is possible only in idyllic parallel universes give in to toasting rum and Coke glasses, and a bootleg box set of *The Adventures of Pete and Pete*.

She laughs at me. Or with me. I can't tell and don't bother to ask.

"So you'll be in New York next week?" she asks.

"All week."

"What's this book fair thing?"

"I don't really know. The press is sending a few of its new authors to stand around and sign a few books. I figured I'd take the opportunity to cash in on my uncle's good graces and crash the city for a while. There's really nothing on television right now."

"That is so true."

"It really is the great existential dilemma of our time."

"Where does he live?"

"My uncle?"

"Yeah."

"Right on Madison Avenue, right in the middle of everything."

"Good. I'll be there on Thursday. You can hide me in your shoes and sneak me into bars."

"They check your shoes now, you know?"

"What?"

"Nothing."

I like freedom.

Later we empty the rest of the bottle of rum, and fall asleep on the floor together watching old Italian horror movies.

. . . .

Two days later, I wake up to a loud thud at the door. A pair of brown boxes sit looking up at the door, expectantly. I open one, and pull out a fresh copy of a book with my name on the cover.

"Hello, freedom."

. . . .

V. NYC Ghosts and Flowers.

For a long time there is nothing; there are only streetlights and tollbooths, evergreens and oaks, rolling roads and the occasional olive off-ramp or white-walled gas station. And then we go under an overpass, and there are lights.

The expectant sigh of the city rings hard in my ears. The symphony of car horns, and the hum of nine million people paying electric bills must be the closest possible combination of notes and textures to the true voice of God. I press my face against the cool glass, desperate to marry the dew on the window, and gently seep through planet Greyhound directly into the concrete-and-steel palm of Heaven.

The first lights belong to the dull green gleam of industrial transformers and rows of blue steel on black water. Then, the dim twilight blush of silver refineries flicker, and the world awakens; thousands of lights stare silently, all lined up like matching metallic chess pieces. Then we sink into another overpass, and the world wakes up into a blindingly endless burst of light.

The Empire State Building's single blue antler sticks up over it all, like an overzealous erection. Beneath its cloud-hold, millions of insomniac little brothers and sisters look up beneath the proud papa of old King Kong movies and modern romantic melodramas, shining, shimmering, twinkling, gleaming, glowing, glistening and sparkling as if each word meant a distinct and unequivocal universe of light.

I get off the bus and cross through the station to 9th Avenue. Three cabs pull over immediately, and wag their tails at the warm fistful of cash I almost lose in the shuffle of guardrails and suitcase olympics. I take the first in line, fighting the urge to shout, "on Dasher...!"

The cabbie says nothing, but jets out upon vague instruction, leaping dozens of potholes in a single bound. We pass fifteen perfume stores accessorized with ten thousand bums and six million hotdog vendors.

At the corner of 92nd I ring the bell and am buzzed into Jack's six-story apartment house.

I wrestle away the impossibly heavy door, and step inside the slowest elevator in Manhattan. I am counting the ceiling tiles. 46. 47. 48. I am naming them. Walter. Sally. Horatio.

When the elevator blinks open an hour and a half later, I'm immediately swallowed into the bright parade of fresh alien artifacts Jack has arranged for me. He hands me a glass of wine, and whisks me into a deck of cards and a large pile of videotaped interviews of dead American authors from the 1960s. By day, Jack is a successful stockbroker, but after dark he is to art what Willy Wonka is to chocolate.

We finish the wine, and I have two beers, an ice cold glass of scotch that smells like smoked salmon, and several packs of the most expensive baseball cards in Manhattan. Jack starts talking about music, newly jailed family members, and his latest series of LSD-fueled English cliff diving competitions. I screw my head back on and nod.

In the living room, overlooking the cross section between Central Park and what he tells me is Woody Allen's apartment, I am coerced into doing a reading from my latest novel about collecting too many baseball cards and falling too fast in love in the great American small anytown. The pages are blurry and stuck together, and the words fall out of my mouth with the terrible grace of a cotton hailstorm. But when I finish, Jack smiles the bright new toy smile of a six-year-old, and claps gleefully.

"It's getting there," he says. "It's really getting there!"

Two beers and thirty uneasy steps later, I finally retire to the guest room. I pull myself up to the window, and look out one last time on the dim, gloaming magnificence of my very own New York City bedroom window, wondering how I can corner Woody in a coffee shop in the morning.

. . . .

I wake up the next day, completely unaware of the concept of hangovers, and head immediately to Washington Square Park.

And I love this place. Some whisper that this little cutout is old, tired, overused, robbed, raped, deloused and commercialized. I say people still go to Paris, Rome, London, and the supermarket. I say, my mother is older, more commercialized and less hip than she's ever been, but I still go see her on birthdays, holidays, and all those days in between when I happen to run out of cash.

I hoof it to 86th and Lexington, and take the subway. Nobody really rides the buses, but everyone rides the subway; old men ride the subway; girls in canvas skirts ride the subway; opera singers live in subway bench apartments with great greasy-haired Hispanic guitar players.

Old women ride the subway. Why aren't they all getting married? I want so desperately to be a groomsman!

Poodles ride the subway. Boxes on wheels ride the subway. Pigeons ride the subway. Snapping turtles and teenagers with broken legs ride the subway.

I stroll into Jackson Square, buy a Coke from a less-than-jolly white-haired Italian cart dweller, and have a seat on the nearest slab of stone I can find. I wonder who else sat here, in this very spot. Bogart? Kerouac? Whitman? Pauly Shore?

Old white men sleep here now. Pink mothers with pink towels on blue strollers roll by. Middle-aged black men in denim shirts and white ball caps circle the circle.

Pigeons have their local 401 meetings here; they coo with all the impressed vibrato of a shivering baby opera singer.

And Jesus Christ, does New York have big fucking dogs! They're everywhere! they sit calmly on maroon leashes while their owners sniff each other's cell phones; they have thick auburn hair and great big dinosaur feet. They smile with their Oscar night red carpet tongues and nod upwards with surgically-altered cat ears.

8th Avenue to Bleeker Street; Abingdon Square.

Canes, cups, pigeons, warriors, mosquitoes, swing sets, old women with gigantic black rectangular glasses, windsocks and backpacks all go dancing.

Bleeker Playground.

Chartreuse and lavender shirts slide and swing gleefully against the backdrop of bored busied parents who distract themselves by sniffing each other's dog's cellphones

Biography Bookshop, 400 Bleeker Street.

An old man sits in the corner abusing a young dog. A bald man, 6'7" or so, wearing a green trench coat, gazes stone-eyed at the gay and lesbian section to my right; A frowning girl with coarse black Russian hair kneels by the drama section on my left. I buy a paperback copy of an unpronounceable Dostoyevsky novel, and no one shoots at me.

Christopher Street and 7th Avenue.

In Christopher Park, stone people and heavily animated lawyers look for Washington Street, speaking incautiously in wild accents. No pigeons have landed as of yet.

The aeroplane flies high, looks left, bears right.

Greenwich and Charles.

A hundred grinning kids play with a rainbow parachute behind a two-story chain-link fence. They kick dull red rubber balls toward the street, but can't quite make it over.

On the other side of the street, the bag from *American Beauty* hangs in the air; it's a little older now, and is beginning to turn brown. I say hello anyway and head south.

Ambulances cannot play the trumpet.

Poor old Greenwich. *Starbucks, Apple, Barnes and Noble, Supercuts.* Wait—rich old Greenwich!

A mother pushes an empty stroller while her little boy—maybe three—pedals a tricycle backwards down the sidewalk on the Avenue of the Americas. One day, he will surely be president. I ask for his handprint.

"Trikeee!" he says triumphantly.

A white man passes a black bum on a bike.

Bum: What's that?
Bike: CD player.
Bum: What?
Bike: CD PLAYER!
Bum: Wanna sell it?
 Bike: No.
Bum: What?
Bike: NO!
Bum: Oh.

Father Demo Square.

An old man with thinning blue hair gobbles a bag of torn bread as a small army of pigeons clear landing strips and dance violently around him. He slings bits of stale bread to the ground, inciting a mad ballet of birdfeet that peck, toss, kick, and scratch to the melody of nearby cab horns.

The biggest pigeon in New York City tears a chunk from the mother-piece, and sends several crumbs flying towards a little finch. The finch makes a daring catch, and flies to a nearby lamppost where the fatter, slower birds cannot reach him.

The old man empties the entire bag onto the ground and lights a cigarette. His expression reaches a deep, wry satisfaction as his cooing subjects dance around the remaining circus of sneakered feet.

Gobble, peck, shout, lurch, stride, buzz, chew, ponder, frown, gaze, admonish, stare, hum, mumble, buzz, chew, strut, wander.

Selling Out.

At 3:00 I take the subway into Times Square to catch a movie.

I have two large beers and a chicken parmesan sandwich at the café on the second floor, and watch people watching people on escalators being watched.

I watch the prettiest girls that ever lived frowning sullenly, and wrinkling their noses at the odd potpourri of indoor air as they glide off into heaven without even waving goodbye. Or hello.

I watch the wrinkled faces of the past drift by, and crane their necks up in squinted admiration at the breaks of sunlight peaking through the glass ceilings above them. I watch their features becoming smooth, like uncrumpled paper, as they float slowly towards heaven.

I watch people who look tired, who look lonely, who look like glass ceilings, who blink like children fresh from the womb blink; I watch every bodily and facial possibility God has ever erected flutter by my ten dollar sandwich.

Later, on the way back to Jack's apartment, I take a wrong train and have to cross through Central Park to get back to Madison. Fortunately, I pass by even more oversized dogs, pigeons, squeaking playgrounds and chirping children.

I hit the reservoir, and take the jogging path around the outer ring of the park.

Halfway through, I stop to watch the sun easing into its daily disappearing act behind the backdrop of buildings before me, and am frozen dead by the amber glow of it all becoming magnified over the water.

Sparse clouds frame the sun; all the buildings around me look like jagged rows of teeth. The water behind the large wire metal fence in front of me rolls gracefully on, just past the point where the gravel meets the sea meeting the city.

Little glass windows look like distant diamonds. Pretty joggers frown determinedly. Old Jewish men walk by, waving their arms wildly, telling ridiculous stories. I wish I could hear them better; I wish the world had more time and more paper, more teeth.

The clouds come together quickly, like a pair of folding hands. It may rain; it may break. But I love this city. I want to grow old here. I want to die here. I want to write that on something made of stone.

. . . .

On Tuesday, I crawl out of Jack's apartment and take the subway into Times Square. The book fair I'd reluctantly signed up for is nearby on 44th street, but I have no idea in which direction. I pass by the Shubert Theatre, and worry that I've fallen into a completely different dimension; the dizzying blizzard of neon television skyscrapers behind me wave goodbye.

I pass by six hundred and fifty three drugstores. Nothing. I turn around to go backwards.

I slide though a turnstile, and pass the Shubert Theatre from the other side. Brightly colored carnival posters cast cold compass shadows straight down into the grey-brown cracks on the sidewalk. I follow them up the walls, and through the hot steam of subway grates.

I walk back and forth for nearly an hour with a pile of books under my arm, breaking into the occasional cold or hot or freshwater sweat. Little day-glo fish swim by, sucking at the insides of their cheeks.

I am counting things I find on the streets. Ticket stubs are up by three at the half, but cigarette butts are poised for a big comeback.

Anyone with any sense would have a cell phone, or a seeing-eye dog or a Sherlock Holmes mustache to twirl. I wonder if I could start a fire if hard pressed? I wonder if I could live off of poster-shadows and cigarette butts?

I spin around several more times before finding an information center back in Times Square within a kiosk of computers. One of them tells me I should be at 20 West. I pat it on the head as it jumps into my lap, knocking the pile of books all over the fake marble tile on the floor.

I recognize ****'s bald head from book covers and introduce myself.

"Hey, nice to meet you."

"You too. Ah—do you have any idea what the hell we're supposed to be doing here?"

"We are—supposed to sell several thousand books to all these people, I think."

I look around. There are several dozen other tables. Each one has its own fake marble Mount Rushmore of its own unknown Murderer's Row of next-generation great American novelists. Behind each table sit several confused pigeon-eyed freshwater sweat stained editors and authors, and unlucky brothers-in-law asking what the hell they are doing here. Between the tables and all the confused pigeon eyes, five or six people pace the circular path through the building, each one blinking, pausing, furling eyebrows, and buying nothing.

"Oh. Piece of cake," **** says.

We stand behind our table, pretending to be impressive fake marble statues for an hour or so before *** shows up and loses his own stack of freshwater-marked books on the floor.

"Hi," he says extending a giant fake marble handshake, "sorry I'm late. I slept in a little, and then got kind of lost. What did I miss?"

"Well, we've sold 58 books so far," **** says.

"Really?"

"No, not really. We haven't sold a thing."

"We haven't even talked to a thing," I say.

"Oh. Wow that's too bad."

"Hey, you didn't bring a flare gun by any chance, did you?"

"Sadly, no. But I do have this." *** says, as he slams a fifth of whiskey loudly onto the table.

"Even better. You brought charisma!"

Within fifteen minutes, we are talking to everyone, selling a book a minute and signing autographs while tap dancing.

"Have you guys met *****?"

Neither of us has.

"I did a reading with him in D.C.," **** says.

"Really? I read his book. It's fucking fantastic."

"That's because he has six fingers."

"He has…"

"He's the six fingered man. I call it the genius finger. I think that's the reason his books are fucking *fantastic*."

"You ever see that old Twilight Zone episode…"

"Exactly. He's skipped an entire step in the evolutionary process."

"OH! Does he have a giant swollen head?"

"No."

"A silver cape?"

"No. He's not that far ahead. He can't make things move with his mind—yet. But he has evolved just enough to be able to write award-winning novels."

"And publish our crap."

"Even the beneficiaries of evolutionary mutations have their faults."

*** assures a squinting middle-aged woman in a long navy blue dress two sizes too large that his book will indeed cure her rheumatism. She hands him fifteen dollars.

. . . .

New York and Cubism

On Wednesday, I play with Jack's kids and watch the local news until noon.

The Guggenheim is just a short walk from 92nd street. The gallery is featuring a spiral of Brazilian works and important 18th century religious art painted on wooden panels removed from old churches. Only- I'm not interested in any of this.

Farther in, Picasso and Braque deconstruct mandolins and coffee tables into perfectly sliced pieces of measured brown and black paint. Nothing looks at all out of place, even though everything has been mutated, warped, stretched and rearranged.

I wonder how you can look at the world and tear it apart so correctly? It's madness—it's angular and random—but you couldn't improve upon a single brushstroke. I wonder if I could ever tear apart the world so beautifully.

All around me, people stop and mumble in every language imaginable, much more so than in any other section of New York I've ever been to; they all stare so hard at the beautifully deconstructed brushstrokes laid out before them. They all seem as mystified as I am.

If only they'd look so mystified at the sidewalks outside, at the hot dog vendors and gigantic dogs, at the escalator teeth and subway belly; if only they'd stop to smell the subway grates! If only they'd look at life with such delicately furled brows.

But, then there would be no reason for me to be here, reporting on the cracks in the tile floor of the Guggenheim by Picasso's *Accordionist*. I trace each line as they casually flake off into drops of Monet colors dripped in Pollock precision, oblivious.

Some of the cracks belong on the wall with the all the paintings. What is the difference, after all, between the brushstroke and the bootsole?

Outside, I swim through an ocean of machine sweat. Shopping bags, orange stands, subway grates, chocolate labs, pretty girls in dark sunglasses and biped furniture drift off in the distance. An old German couple asks me, "Please—supermarket in the street—number?" I shake my head, sadly.

All the people look like confetti.

Beautiful half-naked women hang on the sides of telephone booths. Black girls, white girls, yellow girls, auburn girls, pale girls, electric blue girls, transparent girls, mother girls, daughter girls, and invisible voyeur girls blink by and flutter off.

At two o'clock, I manage to find the Marriott with time to spare, walking straight in before spotting a mirror and noticing how much I look like Spike Lee at a Klan meeting.

Everything and everyone is bright and still. I take the elevator to the eighth floor bar, and pretend invisibility.

Fountains, suits, slacks, sports coats, marble tile, red paper lanterns, golden mobiles, black stewardesses, Van Gogh carpet, floors stacked like Aldous Huxley hives and golden, shimmering guard rails stare me down and assert my true place in the overall capital scheme of things.

Neon Disney colors spin around me in awful blurs—teal, azure, cobalt, lavender, magenta, and polished copper swing off the curls of my eyelashes.

Triangles, squares, spheres, snail shells, and deco clash with outright Cubism. I get dizzy.

"Hey—Charlie!"

I look up. Jack is waving down at me from the ninth floor guard rail. A split-second later, he appears in his grey business suit wearing a typically mischievous Jack smile.

"Hey! How's it going today?"

"Pretty good so far…"

"What've you been up to?"

"Well, I went to the Guggenheim…"

"Oh great. Great. Hey—do they still have that big gold thing right in the—ah—center?"

"That reaches up through four floors? Yeah."

"Did you check out the Brazilian exhibit?"

"Not really. I was more into the permanent collection."

"Yeah, that's good stuff…"

Jack proceeds to tell me the complete architectural history of the Guggenheim. He knows who built every building in New York. He knows, even, who installed the chipped, yellow fire hydrant on the corner of 5th and 42nd.

I'm waiting for a waitress. My brain is caught between whiskey and a beer, but no one ever comes.

"Listen, I should get back," Jack says, fighting off a mischievous grin.

We both stand up.

"How do you walk around in places like this? I can't imagine having a business meeting, or—Christ—sleeping!"

"This is my life, Charlie."

"You live in a fucking Kubrick film."

"Yeah. Heh. You should—you should see—ah—some of the places in Japan..."

"Yeah. I'll get right on that."

"I'll see you tonight, Charlie."

Jack shakes my hand, and turns into a bright neon puff of smoke.

. . . .

In Her Best Patti Smith Voice.

I meet Claire at Penn Station the next day. We hide all her worldly possessions under a park bench, and head south.

"So, how did the book thingy go?" she asks.

"It was horrible until we discovered firewater. Then, there was a laser light show and a really impressive demonstration on table dancing. I didn't know I had it in me."

"No?"

"Yeah, sure. It was great. Shit, I probably sold enough books to buy two whole bags of almonds in Central Park."

"Really?"

"Seriously! Maybe even three."

"I know what we're doing tomorrow."

We talk the doorman at a bar on Bleeker Street into believing Claire has forgotten her identification, and push our way towards an abandoned piano in the back.

"Can we sit here? Oh, look, the keys are fossilized!"

"What should we drink?" Claire asks, her right eyebrow slightly menacing.

101

"Alcohol. The alcoholic kind."

"You're so smart, Charlie."

"Yeah. Well, I did go to college."

I order a pair of rum and Cokes, and fight my way back to Claire. Her features act like lighthouse sweeps in the dim bar-light; she catches me staring more often than she should.

"Oh, watch the band," she growls.

"They're fucking horrible. Is this Third Eye Blind?"

"No, it's the Verve Pipe."

"Same thing."

"Pretty much."

"Are they filming a VH1 special?"

"*I love the shitty 90's?*"

"Part deux. Want another?"

"Please."

I get another round of drinks. Claire is busy prying keys off of the piano.

"What are you…?"

"They have to be stopped. People have limits," she says, launching a fossilized piano key toward the stage.

"Holy shit! Nice throw..."

"FUCK THE NINTIES! PLAY SOME VELVET UNDERGROUND!"

"You really must meet my parents."

"Shit, I think I hit one of them!"

"My parents?"

"The band."

"Quick, the back door. Fuck! I think the bass player saw you..."

"Serves him right. Fucking Hootie and the fucking Blowfish. PICK ANOTHER DECADE, ASSHOLES!"

We gather ourselves, and rent a space on a bus bench.

"Oh well. It's morning somewhere," Claire says, exhaling a cartoon question mark into the midnight air. She looks at me, and notices that I've started playing footsie with myself.

"You're just jealous."

"If only I could fly like a piano key..."

New York should always look like the spaces between nightclubs.

We walk by Washington Square, and I disappear between a homeless person and a statue of Ulysses Grant and piss Picasso's *Guernica*.

"It was a rum and Coke, Charlie..."

"What of it?"

"Hold on..." Claire walks off into the shadows and crouches down.

"What are you..."

"You don't think it's sexist that you can do that and I have to hold it in?"

"What's wrong with being..."

"IST! IST! You've just never been a woman. I checked. Wait—there's more..." She walks between two college kids, licking one on the chin. "Sex?" she asks. They stop walking and start babbling. She laughs and spins around.

"Are you crazy?"

"Ist! Wait—what? That? This? It's just a word. God—you're all so fucking easy! Sex! SEX!"

A hippy kid with a worn canvas backpack whirls around. "What are you two walking around on?"

"Stereotypes."

The kid proceeds to give a sermon on the party of the octade, scribbling addresses, phone numbers and directions on the back of a less-than-flattering caricature of Catherine the Great.

"SEX!" she shouts in her best Patti Smith voice.

A drag queen walks by and tips her pencil eyebrows at me curiously. "She just came this way," I tell it.

"I see."

"Honey, lets go home and take your medicine…"

"It's just a fucking word, Charlie."

"Are you trying to demonstrate something? Is there a point, or did I lose a bet?"

"The point is…"

"Fuck it. Hey, is this NYU?"

"I don't know. Probably…" I pull out a sharpie from my inside coat pocket and write *fuck it* 642 times on the faded brick wall until it all starts to look like Cubism.

We get a cab back to Jack's, and tumble up six flights of stairs. "I think they're asleep," Claire whispers.

"I think they went to sleep six hours ago. Scotch?"

"Yeah…"

On the couch there is a misunderstanding of fingers, legs, arms, lips, bait, tackle, rivers, when I'm an old woman I'll wear chartreuse, jazz horn, shirt buttons, bars on windows, television, elapsed time footage, cigarette breath, collapsing eyes, wonder, confusion, cricket symphonies, Moonlight Sonata, sidewalk flowers, choir brick, front-facing bra straps, the skin underneath skin, honey and salt, frost and ginger, sweat and pancake mix, orange peel, drum solo, the nape of her neck, sudden street steam, sighs, rose poems, her best Kim Gordon voice—

"Charlie? charlie…"

"Why'd you say it lowercase?"

"I'm already seeing someone."

"I don't see anyone."

"Charlie, I can't. You can play with my tit all night, but it's…"

"Wow. You get right to the point…"

"Charlie, I—goodnight Charlie. I'm going…"

Lips meet and dissipate in the doorway. I watch their naked shadows wander and lick the scotch from my teeth.

I am left with images of leaves falling, or the smell of burning film. I am left free, happy and light, confused and old; I am left vibrating alone.

There are no sounds left in the world—only movement. I follow the footsteps in my brain, across the uncombed hair on graves, to bed.

Goodnight orange peels and barflowers. Goodnight shadow people. Goodnight sweet, acidic, Penelope, Nausicaa, Liz Phair, carbon paper, wax hearts, candy eyes, bullet tongues, bad ideas and happy accidents. Goodnight cartoon light bulbs, human doubt, pianokeys and parkblossoms. Goodnight fiberglass stars.

In the morning, I finish both of our leftover glasses of scotch, smoke three cigarettes, open a pack of baseball cards, and see a six-foot-five white rabbit walking down a random path in central park. Jack's kids don't blink, but Claire assures me it is real.

In the afternoon, I walk her to the bus station and say goodbye, lipless.

. . . .

Scat on, White Man.

I wander down by the United Nations building on 47th Street. Someone is setting up a small row of folding chairs for world peace.

Three feet away, a crowd gathers around what looks like a giant farmer's market.

Four elderly, frail-looking women frown at the thousands of different skin tones all dressed up in the same sharp black suit.

A Chinese woman does tongue triplets on a cell phone; a tall Russian man eats an apple.

A small crowd of Mexican women gather around a large cavalcade of disembodied car seats, doing Elmo impersonations for a series of small, scrunched kid-faces.

I can't make out the rest. There are white, black, auburn, crème brulè, brown eyes, neon blue-green, dark sunglasses, Yankee caps, beards, legs, teeth, briefcases and umbrellas. None of them seem too outwardly upset over war, world banks, terrorist sleeper cells, or some vision of the overreaching arm of western influence; everyone walks by quietly and into the blender.

Is a small Japanese man with an overzealous camera and an "I love NY" shirt a sign of overreaching? Are a pair of Yugoslavian men with spiffy haircuts a sign? They're not looking for land mines in the sand.

Am I still caught up on the surface of appearances? Maybe I should talk to the next Palestinian I see.

"Hi. Excuse me sir, do you think we're fucked as a nation?"

Do you think he'd respond?

"I'm sorry son, I have to run. I have theatre tickets and my wife is a bitch about lateness."

"Landmines? Hamas?"

"I've already eaten, thanks."

Would it go like that?

All these people really want is a nice loaf of bread, a bag of peaches, a pint of organic yogurt, and a couple of knishes thrown into a nice little square box.

My bones hurt from the half-week spent here. New York is a stiff mistress. My right foot is burned charcoal black, but I don't mind so much. Everything here is aching, building, growing, growling, grating, rushing, pushing, howling, raking, shirking, shaking, hammering, and turning to back into the basic building blocks of life. Even the air—even the metal and wood and soot here—changes and blends and becomes a magnificent parody of itself.

Movie times at the AMC on 42nd and 7th secured, I take buses, legs, and directions from strangers back to Washington Square. It's still a little too early and a little too weekaday for jazz I suppose, but there are still plenty of skateboards and hotdog vendors. And there are plenty of pretty young things opening books that—somehow—I can't talk to. *Women* women are intimidating enough, but New York women?

It shouldn't even matter. Does it? I'm here. I'm alive, and I'm prepared to propose to the sidewalk despite everything.

I open a fresh copy of my own fresh book, and become my own pretty little unapproachable thing.

A gleefully reprehensible jazz band begins playing in the background on a makeshift particleboard stage a hundred yards away. They've got a nice little rhythm section, but the large, mulleted guitarist playing smooth jazz chords and clean simple scales makes me want to throw fossilized piano keys. He sways a bit, but not quite enough. And—

Oh god! He's trying to sing! The mulleted swaying white man is trying to scat! This is Washington Square! I know I'm not in a Henry James novel or a Corso poem, but still—I'm a little let down. In fact, I want a divorce.

In fact, I'm only kidding. Scat on white man. You look like you're having fun enough, and I'm far enough away to ignore you. Someone throw me a fucking hotdog.

A little blonde girl in a light blue skirt and matching blouse sits down on the left corner of my stone stump, and pulls a sandwich from a brown paper bag. One day I will surely grow a tongue.

They really aren't bad, the hundred-yard off particle board band. The drummer's left hand does all sorts of impressive skips on the ride, and the whole lot of them cut in and out of a number of Brazilian and Cuban themes rather nicely. It just isn't dangerous enough.

Maybe that's what I'm aiming fossils at; there's no element of struggle in the sound. I miss that. I need that. I like art that struggles; I like jagged paint, and brash horns blowing from blue faces. I like strained voices. I like contorted, impossible sentences. Obviously.

The drummer rolls on. He could probably play this stuff in his sleep. I could certainly listen to it while I slept.

The little blonde girl in front of me lights a cigarette.

"Scuze me?" I lean forward, and see her scribbling frantically in a small, pocket-sized notebook. "Excuse me? D'you have an extra smoke?"

"Oh no, this is my last one. Sorry." She flips open the pack as if to prove its emptiness.

"No problem. Thanks."

Also, she is a little less than I thought she might be. Her face has either too much or not enough Cubism. I will decide later.

A giant grinning swordsman with leathery skin and a black cape imitates a matador loudly in the center of the park. I move to investigate.

A few people start to clap. One yells, "bravo!" as he dodges an imaginary bull and sings, "merci bo quo!"

Several sleeping guitar players strum sleepy classic rock chords from the fringe of the stone circle where the matador's centered. They play with half the bravado of the bull fighter, but with none of the comic irony. Others rest, or read, or sunbathe, or frown blankly with their eyes closed, dreaming of sandals and salty shellfish.

A man in the audience starts to chant at the matador, "Cut orange! Cut orange! Cut orange!"

The matador stops and stares, obstinately. He approaches the man with a new seriousness and, happily, an orange. He hands it to the man and directs with his fingers, "this is the sight. This is the trigger. Sight. Tigger. Got it?"

"Yeah!"

"This—people—is a beginning. Just bear with me, and there will be an end! Cutting an orange is no show; cutting three oranges is! Do I have any volunteers?" One man, middle aged and chuckling, steps forward. Another, a young woman, is pushed. The matador brings them together.

"This is the sight. This is the trigger. Sight. Trigger. Got it? Yes? Good!" He steps back and inspects the ring.

"You—you stand here. You stand here. You stand here. Good. Now—you have a window, a window this big." His bony index finger draws a small square around his face. "At the center of the window is the nose."

The three volunteers begin throwing practice oranges in awkward underhand jerks at the matador. Everyone throws low.

"No. No. No! The *window* is my nose. Remember—this is the sight. This is the trigger. Now, you stand here. You stand here. You stand here. The window is my nose..."

He returns to the center and addresses the crowd, "Ladies and gentleman, this will come only one time, so I'd advise you all to keep your eyes open. Now—I am going to give you something you have not seen, felt, or heard before! I give you—the spirit of the sword!"

The matador holds up a large, plain looking wooden sword. The audience laughs.

Meanwhile, three black kids careen down the side of the circle on a red scooter. One of them shouts, "hey Hector—you gonna waste these peoples' time much longer?"

"Please do not rush me!" Hector turns and faces the crowd. "Now I need your attention—and a dollar." The audience laughs.

The kids continue, as if in a Greek chorus, "someone told him he's talented!"

"Someone was mistaken!"

Hector continues, "ladies and gentleman—you know what I do for a living—and to tell you the truth—I am not living. So give generously!"

"Just cut the damned orange!"

"I want you all to give a dime, a nickel, a quarter, a dollar…"

"An orange!"

"A few dollars…"

"It's hard to believe that out of eight million sperm cells, you were the winner!"

Poor Hector doesn't finish cutting the oranges. Instead, he walks around collecting dimes and quarters into a brown burlap sack. When he's finished, he walks into the center of the ring, and gathers his things.

"There is no future in swordsmanship!" he cries.

The matador bows, and a few people clap.

"Do you understand that you're messing with three very large young black men?"

"He's got a sword!" I yell.

"He's got a wooden sword! That's just a step up from a stick. I think we can take a damned stick!"

The leader of the chorus chuckles, "if you see half-a wooden sword lying around tomorrow in Washington Square, you'll know who did it!"

The three very large young black men start their show, flipping and break-dancing for twenty minutes over a boombox chorus of cheesy eighties pop and hip hop, telling jokes between breaths.

At the end, they ask for four volunteers. One of them, remembering my earlier brashness, grabs me by the hand and leads me to the middle, adding, "this fucker'll do!"

"WE—people! Listen! We are going to jump all four of these people—but we need your help. Now— we could jump them now—but then you could split. So we're going to take your money first!"

They go around the circle collecting for a few moments, and after the initial gratitude has dried up, they play the neighborhood card.

"Hey, who was the last to give? You sir, where are you from? Brooklyn! Alright! Hey Greenwich, you gonna let that happen?"

"I've got two dollars!"

"Two dollars! Two dollars! Harlem, you gonna let that happen?"

"I've got a quarter!"

"A quarter! Harlem has a quarter! New Jersey you gonna let that happen?"

"I've got a dollar!"

"A dollar! Where are you from, sir?"

"Hoboken!"

"Hoboken! Damn, Bronx, you gonna let that happen?"

A young woman throws another dollar into the bag.

"Where you from, m'am?"

"Pakistan."

"Pakistan! Iraq, you gonna let that happen?"

Finally they walk back into the center. "You two—the two guys, get the hell out of here, we were just kidding." The audience laughs. I sit down, relieved.

The chorus asks the remaining girls to bend over for a prolonged period, "for inspiration," then jumps them successfully.

. . . .

It's raining in the wide-windowed world of Manhattan. Umbrellas and long johns march together in the streets in tight, sullen lines. Today the pace is up, the eyes are down, and the dewy shopping bags from department stores are tucked a little more securely into the stiff cracks of arms.

I join the game, tripping around on my first New York blister, a little angrier, a little more guarded, and a little more invincible.

I hoof it through the rain towards 266 West 47th Street, where there's supposedly an entire museum devoted to New York jazz. There isn't. There's not even a 266 West 47th. There's a 268, but it's a drugstore.

No matter. I am large; I contain multitudes.

A few streets down, I find a photography gallery showcasing the best black and white impressions of drag queens, bums, alleys, patriots, Bogarts, and window panes the city has to offer.

Other cities and states are represented as well, but are sparser. Pennsylvania is a strained family vacation

113

in a small coughing car. Arkansas is a wide, open field of wheat. Memphis and Laredo are swimming pools.

Wyoming is a bleeding highway; Montana, a bone-dry ranch. Wisconsin is a rain-soaked road and an unlucky dog.

Northern California is full of redwoods, thrift shops, and children with sad eyes, wild hats, and no hair.

White Sands is just that—plus a woman looking to be an extra in a John Waters movie, complete with horn-rimmed glasses and an ill-fitting white dress.

Vegas is a brooding child standing on a marble floor. L.A. is a department store where children sit on the floor looking through primitive wood-paneled television screens.

Arizona is a car window and a dusty gulch. El Paso is a house going by on wheels.

Utah is a lonely little girl and a telephone pole. Portland is a skating rink.

L.A. returns as a honeycombed planet of airline luggage, and possibly where all misfit socks go after disappearing through the dryer.

Greater Texas is still a cowboy state. In fact, Fort Worth has them all bronzed.

Dallas is a bank overflowing with cars. San Marcos is a secret meeting in a diner in a David Lynch film.

Cincinnati is full of old women with flags and squash-faced babies sleeping in the arms of mothers, fathers, and old black taxicabs.

Candlestick Park is always being emptied. Palo Alto is a big green monster.

Forest Lawn Cemetery is both a day at Disney World and a Greek Tragedy.

Venice Beach is for muscles.

Hot Springs is all eyes and Marilyn Monroe dresses.

Pigs swim in Aquarena Springs.

Some of the pictures are in color; they glow with neon and halogen Jesuses, blue skies, and canary-yellow dresses over white teeth, long rows of evergreen forests, beach fires, and bright white sediment.

Other cities have circuses complete with wire clowns and girls in short skirts with big umbrellas, three rings, two squares, old wood-wheeled wagons, colossal tents, and naked flatbed trucks. And elephants—maybe two-dozen or more. And all at once.

Somehow all of it—all the women in ballerina bathing suits, and all the men in their old war clothes—somehow all of it looks to me like a giant birthday cake built for the 1930s. Hello America! We see you, still.

And then there's Ground Zero in full, horrifying color. Goodbye, America.

Firemen gouge their eyes with handkerchiefs, and splash handfuls of water to fight off the smoke and tears.

Straight streets become angular grey fogs. One photo is nothing but smoke and a pair of American flags. And dust—dust that is equal parts man and stone and steel and desks and jewelry, boots, picture frames, grocery lists…

I can hardly look.

One photo says,

NUKE
Them
All

in ash in a window.

Buildings are nothing more than skeletons. People, still, are still forever, and even those walking in now—removed by so many years—perhaps never witnessing a second of this live—are looking on just as choked and still as those we lost.

Outside, life goes on. A young black man nods at me knowingly, as several suits poke my freshly-soaked head with the steel tips of their umbrellas waiting for the bus on Fifth. I light a cigarette and stare down at the ashes I make.

On the bus, a frazzled mother steps hard on my toes, chasing after her curly-headed little two-year-old. She apologizes, but I tell her I don't mind. I'll take the accidents of frazzled mothers over distracted suits any day.

Back outside, a woman, maybe thirty-five, jogs down Fifth Avenue in black bicycle shorts and a worn, grey Nike t-shirt. I look for the camera crew following her, but can't find one. I decide sometimes *life* is an ad for life.

I find a pub near Bleeker Street with a little red "open" sign hung over a rather inconspicuous doorway.

The inside walls are painted blacker than deep space, and adorned with several large tile paintings of Jimi Hendrix, Mick Jagger, Keith Richards, and Elvis Costello. I think I've found a home.

I'm starving, and by now feeling more than a little lost, but I manage to open a book and keep myself occupied while the bartender is busy watering down a flock of loud, young Englishmen.

When the place clears out a little, the old man approaches me and apologizes over a pleasant rain of "sirs" and "pleases." I tell him, "no worries," order a pint, and ask for a menu.

There's a stage at the front of the club with a couple of monitors, a folded-up drum kit, and a huge silver amplifier.

"How often do you have bands in here?"

"O—bout seven days a week, sir. That's what this place is all about."

"I love the art in here. Costello and Hendrix…"

"Sure. We used to have a fellar in here who played with Jimi Hendrix himself. Shame though—he went off the same way."

"That's rock 'n roll for you."

"Sure is, sir. But look, you really should come back and hear the place do what it was built for."

"I'm sure I will. Thanks."

I order another beer and a burger, "burnt to a crisp," and light up a smoke as The Supremes version of "Rolling on the River" kicks on over the stereo. The bartender strolls by and offers to buy me another pint. I think of changing my address right there.

They've even got old 45s hung up on the bathroom wall behind a layer of thick dusty glass. I spot "Leaving on a Jet plane," something by *Squeeze* and "Witchy Woman" by *The Eagles*.

I take care of the check, and walk out towards a record store I spotted earlier to pick up the double disc Paul Westerberg bootleg sitting neatly in the window.

"$32.49"

"Here you go. Hey—which way's Broadway? Left?"

"No—you go up from here. North."

"Thanks."

The air outside is 800° below what it was just five minutes ago, and the rain is really coming down now. A plane flying over Manhattan might think they were watching some strange ballet involving the synchronizing of millions of black umbrellas opening all at once.

I hop the Broadway line and ride it a few stops before realizing that I've been going in the wrong direction. Again.

By now, I can't just turn around and go back; there are too many one-way streets and alien archways. I'm lost. I'm lost, and I'm a new level of cold.

And for the first time, I know what it is to be a real New Yorker. I don't look up. I don't take cabs. I don't ask for directions. If I get lost, I figure it the fuck out, even when all the happy little paint-by numbers streets have turned into something resembling Chinese subtitles.

I've long abandoned the idea of using logic to navigate this city anyway. Whatever blueprint they originally dreamed up for this place was swallowed by King Kong and coughed back out into a blender.

I don't speak to strangers.

I am a real New Yorker. I don't take cabs. My feet hurt. I've got no right heel left, and no left toe. I have no eyes, on account of the rain. My skin is now

97.684 percent water. I have six assholes that all shit carbon copies of myself that are all miserably lost.

The bag in my left hand is torn at the bottom, middle, top, left and upper right corner. In fact, it can no longer be called a bag at all. It looks more like wet confetti than a bag.

I am a real New Yorker. I walk over sewer grates, even though they smell like death must smell, because they're slightly warmer than sidewalks.

I am a real New Yorker. Where Whitman would loaf and invite, I simply loathe. I am moody and unapproachable. I hate everyone who's ever worn khaki pants and carried a large black umbrella on a by-name basis.

I am a real New Yorker. I don't buy cheap plastic raincoats on street corners, and I scowl at people who use *real* umbrellas. At night, I sneak into their apartments and steal their Christmas trees.

When I finally make the subway, about a week and a half later, I even want to kill the street performers. A little black kid in high-top sneakers and red-netted shorts blows a smooth sax scale near the 4 train, but I'm tired and aggravated and wet, and I couldn't give a fuck if he was any good. In fact, if I could make one wish on this planet right now, it would wish for a pocketful of change to jam the mouth of that fucking horn. Or, better yet, I could choke the fucker to death with subway stubs. He could keel over right now and I'd clap.

I am a real New Yorker. I piss openly in central park. I walk along the jogging track in the rain with a handful of confetti and a wet cigarette dangling from my swollen bottom lip.

I yell at the bicycle shorts that use me to time laps. "Go ahead—you're all going to have fucking heart attacks at 38, you SAD FUCKS!"

I am a real New Yorker. The skin between my legs in completely gone. No amount of talcum powder can bring that back. And I'm still not taking a fucking cab.

And I still love this city. It's defiant. It's ludicrous. And it's absolutely beautiful. Raw skin and warm piss and no legs and no eyes and bad lungs aside. I love the ducks in the harbor that don't give a fuck about joggers or rain. I love the buildings that don't give a fuck about the rain. I love it all despite my pathetic little misfit bad attitude, and soaking wet Marlboro cigarette.

I love New York. I still love the skyline from Central Park. I still put out all my smokes in my pockets before I'd ever dream of leaving them to rot on the ground.

. . . .

In the morning, there are a thousand things echoing in my head.

I'm thinking of developing a color alert system to warn people away from my bad moods.

"Hiya Charlie, how're you feeling today?"

"Well, to tell you the truth Jack, I'm a little orange."

"Oh man, I'm sorry to hear that. Oh, look at the time! I've really gotta go!"

Downtown, I see a man in plaid golf shoes and think about reporting him. He could be an evil doer. Or a Scotsman.

I get off the subway at Penn Station. A few street vendors are selling bootleg DVD's with Japanese subtitles. Others sell belts, sunglasses, religions, and pornography. One corner smells like a Cuban's ransom in cigars. Another smells like smoky Chinese food. Another, like sweat and pavement.

I look up at the United Nations building, and realize I've gone the wrong way. Again. Backwards through the sweat and pavement, smoky Chinese food, sweat and cigars.

I am getting used to being lost, and I've never been fucking happier. Maybe I *should* move here. Even my interior monologues are cursing.

Cabbies, car alarms, MTV, Jennifer Lopez, cops, traps, whistles, bars, barricades.

I hop the subway to 18th and 7th. Inside the cars, there are advertisements for foot doctors and dentists, network comedies and "a delicious blend of cognac and fruit juices."

Outside, I follow a girl in baggy green pants past a series of drugstores, book stores, cigarette shops, and pizza stands. Eventually, she leads me straight into Washington Square Park, whereby I am immediately propositioned.

"Want some smoke?"

I nod no.

"What?"

"No thanks!"

The girl and her baggy green pants are gone, but off to the right is the faint sweeping sound of a saxophone:

doo—lah—tru-hoop— ho-lah-tru-doop— wee— hee-hee-hee—tru-lah-do-loop—hoo—da-la-loop—

*loot—loot—sco-da-tra-loop—hoo—hoo—hoo-do-tra-
loop— hoo—hoo—oo—ah—ah—oo—tru-la-ta-doop*

He blows the ground apart; breathes like John Henry swings a hammer. Then he pulls back, gracefully, like a golden feather falling to the ground. Then he shatters the pavement with bright tenor notes.

He swings on a tree branch. He flips, sails, hangs, slugs and drops:

oo—ah-oooo—do-loo-de-hoop

An elderly man joins him on trumpet, playing slow, soulful Louis Armstrong yelps through a white muzzle:

*trep-heh—waw-heh—tweet-huh—heh-hare-pa-ah-
lay trep-ha hoo-hoo—scoo—trep-scoo-hoo-ha—
broo-ha—*

The old man is more thoughtful and ragged; he's the slow, subtle blues of the Great Depression, or of archaic, humid-heavy, slow-lit southern back porches.

He's no match for the tenor, who blows like an excited hurricane that rains until there is no land and no air left to rain; who consumes oxygen like a flame; who rages until there is no rage left. The old man knows this and lays back, instead dropping soulful hints just underneath the surface of the water, only occasionally opening up the white mute on the bottom of his horn to really let go.

In the center of the Square is my old friend the matador. I hop over the steps, and watch him collect specimens for his oranges.

A girl near the bottom step sheepishly steps forward. Hector hands her the projectile.

"Throw that orange! Hit me right in the nose. Like that. No! That's not my nose. Yes! There we go!

What's your name? Maria? Maria is a beautiful name!"

He leaps into the air and starts dancing like a distinguished madman.

"Clap your hands you lazy people! Wake up I say! Don't get lazy on me—you're going to make me fall asleep. And I'm holding a dangerous weapon..."

The crowd applauds sporadically.

"The swordsman needs sponsorship! Who will come to the aid of Hector the Great?"

A blushing twenty-year-old girl stands up.

"And what is your name?"

"Julie..."

"Here is Jerry!" he shouts.

"It's Julie."

"No, Julie! Julie has volunteered. Come down here I say! Fear—this is—your enemy!"

Julie practices throwing oranges at Don Quixote's head.

"Now I wield this sword—as if it were a real samurai sword. And I will defeat my foes with this sword," he whispers, "and there are many!"

He demonstrates by twirling around and fighting an army of imaginary swordsmen over the sound of something resembling sad laughter.

"And now—now onto the mystical realm of capemanship," he announces as he juggles his tattered black cloak like a bullfighter to something resembling sad laughter.

"Now—it is finally time to cut the oranges!"

Hector enlists another volunteer, making sure to point out exactly where his nose is.

"That's not it! That's my nose. That is well done my dear! What is your name? Melody? Melanie!

Ladies and gentlemen, there is a third volunteer—Melody!"

Now he practices with all three.

"Too low! Too low! Way too low. Okay. Let's hold them all like this. Now once more. Good. Good. Too low Melody!"

"Melanie!"

"Thank you Melody! Now, I will be standing right here; right here I stand. Now here's how it will go: I will count one, two, and three. You will throw the first orange, and I will slice it in two. Then you Melody. Then you Jerry."

"Julie!"

"Right! Now—I am Hector, the swordsman of Washington Square Park. I live here, but I am not really living—if you know what I mean. Now—you will give me your coins in this silver chalice—and your paper in this (Bloomingdale's) bag. And I will begin on this lucky pillar. I have been here a long time. Thank you fair maiden...fair maiden...kind sir...thank you on behalf of the entire association of swordsmanship..."

Twenty-somethings with sketchpads scribble furiously to capture the moment. Young men scratch their burgeoning beards. A policeman frowns with blue folded arms.

Hector meditates silently. Then—

"On my command..."

Mental drum rolls begin. The first attempt fails.

"No good Jerry! To my nose, it's right here..."

He gives further instructions. The second attempt fails.

"To my nose. Right to my nose. Ladies and gentlemen! This is it. Do or die! I need your energy now. Let's get this one right. Right to my nose. To my nose Melody…"

"Melanie!"

Swoop! He takes out two of three oranges in a flash.

"Ladies and gentlemen—this is not easy. This is but a wooden sword—but these are *real* oranges!"

The crowd responds in sporadic applause and something resembling sad laughter.

"Thank you Melody, Jerry…I leave you now to the mercy of your imagination."

Two oranges lay dead on the battlefield.

Not far away, I find a little bookshop on the sidewalk full of dusty classic literary novels and philosophy textbooks. A bright-eyed, toothless old man with a long white beard looks up from behind a long wooden table.

"Looking for anything in particular?"

"Got any Celine?"

"Yeah. Actually, I just got *Journey Into the End of the Night* in yesterday."

"Sweet…"

"In French."

"Fuck."

"Got it in yesterday…"

"Yeah. Thanks anyway."

"Hey, remember what the Chinese say, 'be careful what you wish for."

"I got it."

"But hey—I have a French dictionary and some audio tapes. You could learn…"

"Thanks anyway."

"Any time."

By the time I get back to the park, my tenor is long gone.

. . . .

"You like jazz?" the cabbie asks with enough sincerity to blind a child.

"Yeah, absolutely."

"I take you to jazz. You'll like! Trust me."

I trust him, and soon enough I'm swept through the late night flickering of Manhattan land mines, yellow and quivering, until he finally deposits me on the banks of a large building with the indescribably lovely inscription: *Blue Note*.

I bloom a pair of legs and walk out, fresh, into the streets, through the door, past the twenty dollar cover, and into a bar who's bricks are made of my wildest Jazz Age dreams.

Inside, it is moderately packed. The band plays what the bartender describes as "a seventies revival of a thirties revival," that's so watered down it might be taking place inside an aquarium.

"This isn't your thing, is it?"

"You noticed? Was it the piano key I just threw? What the hell is this anyway?"

"A seventies revival…"

"of a thirties…right. Isn't this the fucking *Blue Note*?"

"Not on weeknights…"

"So—where *should* I be?"

"All right. Look—there's a club—not far from here—called *Smalls*. It's a bit of a hole in the wall but…"

"Now you're speaking my language."

"Right on. So dig—you go out here, turn right, and head towards 4th and 7th. But, really, it's on 10th." I nod at him sideways. "Oh, and you might want to make a stop on the way. They don't have drinks in there, but you can bring whatever you want in. I'd hit a grocery store and stock up on six packs if I were you."

I pay the tab and thank him.

Ten minutes later, I'm inside of *Small's* with an armful of beer.

There's an empty table in the back of the cramped, smoky space. I sit down, open the first born child of my six pack, and slouch backwards while the band begins to blow. And it's perfect. It's grittier than the walls, tighter than the space between people, and smokier than my lungs will be when I die.

The crowd of disembodied heads sways and nods slightly, silent and attentive in every direction. Everything and everyone here is so focused on the music, I can barely stand it.

An army of bottle openers line the barless bar rail that ropes around all the tables. I watch everyone's squinting eyes. I get carried away in a machine gun snare roll that snaps and bounces playfully off the little toms before moving down to the drummer's kick foot with a trio of syncopated cymbal crashes.

At the end of the first song, the trumpet player calls someone's name in the crowd. "This guy," he says, "is the best fucking piano player in Paris. Get the hell up here, man."

The piano player obliges. He sits down and starts, off the ride cymbal, running around a simple chord pattern, adding sparse sentiments here and there until he's turned a three note run into some wild

127

interdimensional slip that the band swings ineffably through, and trounces apart until the only thing left to do is close your eyes to kill off any question of why this is the absolute best place in the entire world.

. . . .

At the end of the last day, I hit the subway and head back towards central park.

Down the bike path, the water raps its salty tongue against the shoreline. I can't tell if the sea is stronger today, or if it's just more nervous.

New York City is again on alert for terrorism. Cops line every other corner. Men in plain clothes stand in front of pizza shops with large, obvious ear pieces.

We've been issued a level four. I'm not sure what that means, but the joggers don't seem to mind. The old men and their wild-arms and flailing stories don't seem to mind. The sunset doesn't mind, or stop in the middle of its golden drapery of architecture. The buildings don't flinch in the stiff wind.

Just before the sun sets, the reflection on the water becomes almost desperately golden, making everything around it equally golden and desperate and beautiful. The water is glassy gold. The grass is amber gold. The buildings are grey-gold. And in the morning, everything will be golden again, and again in the evening; golden sky, golden ground, golden air.

The sun is absolutely blinding, but I believe in a little blindness every now and then.

. . . .

VI. Pop Scene.

I live in a room with seven paintings, two yellowing crates of records, three cheap particleboard bookshelves, a large chest full of old paper, an overflowing CD stand, desk without order, and a bed. All the light in the room is blue, and the ceiling fan is always spinning slowly off its axis.

I live my life under a microscope. I report on my own twitches. I do things, I write them down, I publish them, and people read the results. I'm making the most of my freedom.

I meet people; they ask me what I do. I tell them I am a writer, and that there are consequences.

I don't know if anyone is really honest with me anymore. People are starting to catch on to the fact that the fly on the wall now has a publisher.

Everyone has started to become a caricature. Everyone has developed a cartoon walk, cartoon voices, and cartoon stories. Everyone I meet is exceedingly dramatic and, as a result, my life has become incredibly dull. I used to meet girls and tell them I have blue eyes.

Now I give them even less.

"What do you do?"

"I'm a writer."

"What do you write about?"

"This. I'm publishing an entire series of books about thinly fictionalized conversations I've had with people who ask me what I do."

"Isn't there anything a little more more…"

"No."

"Are there at least vampires?"

"Yes, but they don't have any special powers, and they all look exactly like Seth Rogen."

"Skinn..."

"Nope. Big, fat, gross-as-fuck early Seth Rogen. And no one tells jokes. Ever."

My right leg is constantly sore from tapping. I notice things—I've always noticed things—but now the things I notice are starting to notice back.

"You're all spies," I mutter.

People do things so their actions might become memorable enough to end up on a shelf somewhere. People do things as if I were the executive producer of a new reality show about small towns where people are doing things superficially, which is to say, a reality show. But I can't help thinking all this is a lie; I can't help but wonder how much I am reporting on this new superficiality, and how much I am actually contributing to it.

I live below real infamy, below fame, but right on the underbelly of the great invisible social radar. My bedroom is bathed in green swashes. The blips keep me up at night. I don't have the bank account of a real celebrity, but I do have the local death, lost anonymity, and the pointless elevation of status that's just enough to make people wary, but not quite wary enough to get you laid.

I'm expected to be certain things. I'm expected to live up to the insanity of my own creations. If I go to a party, I'm expected to replant a lighting fixture in the front lawn, rename a random girl after something from an obscure Homeric episode, and bring at least one friend who'll become fucked up enough to do something that'll get us both violently tossed from said party, and possibly arrested.

130

If I visit a relative, it must be a recognized calendar holiday, one that involves no small amount of drinking, and I simply must be either pathologically nostalgic and quiet, or else entirely revolutionary and sullen. Any in-between politeness is sure to be met with confusion, insurgent familial grudges, and, almost certainly a noticeable amount of hate-mail from people whose names I've forgotten.

If I'm out in public, I'd better be standing under a streetlight smoking a cigarette, looking off into some distant blank space with an indescribable look of depth in my eyes, and I'd better have a pack of baseball cards in at least six of my pockets.

If there's a woman, she's required by law to be thin, young, beautiful, and entirely confused. She is also obliged by written contract to be either a student artist or an ironically popular sexual pariah.

Sometimes I get the feeling the entire world around me is about a sixth of a second away from breaking out into a carefully choreographed teen comedy dance routine at any given moment. Freedom is a silly, confusing, uneven, and erratic beast.

I ask strangers and new acquaintances if they'd like to help me rob a liquor store without any inflection or humor. "You can just drive if you're uncomfortable holding a gun," I say. "I mean, someone else can be Nixon."

The few friends who've actually survived my awful caricatures of their frail personas and bad haircuts have retreated with me into this strange, silent film world filled with secret unspoken languages and nervous handshakes. We find ourselves constantly making carefully constructed references to things that less than five people on the entire planet know about—like "windmilling" or "Jesus Fighting." Elaboration beyond a simple archaic allusion seems unnecessary, and this alone gets us ostracized from most companies.

. . . .

I am making the most of my silly, confusing, uneven, erratic beast.

***** is standing under a long tent, which is supposed to be a book fair, looking slightly perplexed. I shake his hand, eager to get a look at the *magicfinger*.

I am staring. He is shorter than I thought he'd be. I am trying not to get caught staring. Is he Indian? Arabic? I am trying not to stare, but I can't help it. There it is!

When you are young, you're told there's a place called Paris, and then one day you're there, but it still doesn't make you stop staring in enamored awe. And now there it finally is, a little offshoot of his pinky, the *magicfinger*, hanging there, whispering,

"this is why...this is why...this is why..."

I gasp that so much genius could be contained in such a small space, in nothing more than a little ghost piece of skin.

**** arrives, and the three of us and the magicfinger have a beer before the convention has properly enveloped us. And then we have another, and then two more, and then **** insists we have a fifth. And then we are drunk.

****'s eyebrows never change. He tells us stories about being raped in the bathroom by a gang of stoners at a Howard Dean convention on Valentine's

Day, and we can't tell whether or not he is joking. The eyebrows sell the lie.

I am staring at my reflection on the top of his pale, awkwardly-shaped head. I am trying not to stare, although I think the tide is starting to going out. Is that a sailboat?

We go to the convention, three young authors with our laptops and Belgian design team made posters locked in plastic rectangles, our books laid out on the table carefully, as if they were the embalmed bodies of our dead children.

A college professor-type walks by, stops, and grins at us the superior grin of a masterfully developed and thoughtfully erudite arrogance. He appears momentarily to be quite near to almost thinking about the possibility of considering the option of coming to grips with the idea of seeming mildly impressed. He examines our collective spines, pauses and mutters, "not bad, not bad. Yes. Hmmmpff." He asks us questions and nods when we tell him non-answers.

****'s eyebrows are patient as gargoyles. I think he is on the verge of selling him the Brooklyn Bridge. The professor pauses and scratches himself proudly. Behind us, a small, quaint-looking Amish family raises a barn.

Several hours later, the professor throws his arms into the air and gasps triumphantly, "ah, but I have no time for reading *this* now," and walks on to the next table. Rinse and repeat.

People like this come by the table all day looking confused, or sorrowful, or scared. "What is *Pretend Genius*?" they ask in hushed voices.

"Eh—it's like real genius, but without the hangover."

"Yeah, we drink, so you don't have to."

"What's this about?"

"About 159 pages."

"The city."

"Having arms."

"The write to have arms."

"It's an eighty thousand word essay on possible anagrams of the word *bookfair*."

"It's a book of plays based loosely around my days as a Lebanese coal miner."

"It's a cookbook for quadruple amputees."

"It's supposed to be an ashtray. Do you think my mother will like it?"

A cameraman follows us around. I tell everyone he is the next Michael Moore, and that we are going to Cannes, whenever Cannes is.

A few literary journals have tables emptier even than ours. I notice a lone Christian author not noticing us. I notice others I don't care to examine.

We play chess, and people ask us how much the chess set is. ***** decides, next time we will sell shiny objects instead and give away free books with every purchase.

"We'll eliminate the middleman."

**** takes to calling me "the beat writer," and one girl coyly asks where my coffee is.

"It's in my other pants." I strangle them both and piss beer.

"What are these?"

"These are called books."

"Mmm! They still have those?"

I feel, at times, like I'm wearing a gaudy Star Wars costume at a comic book convention. In Kentucky. In the middle of August. I shiver a little, and crawl back into my blackshirt.

People come by with manuscripts, and proposals about taking the time to talk to your stuffed animals about the dangers of smoking, and "Ain't it a lovely day for Jesus?"

People ask us questions, as if any of us have the answers to any questions at all. The only thing we can do is entertain ourselves by pretending we're immensely witty and ironical.

"We're just the authors."

"We're just some of the authors."

"We're the sum of all the authors."

Foreheads wrinkle.

"Where's the publisher?" someone asks.

"Seattle."

"Yes. Getting coffee."

"You came down here from Seattle?"

"No, we're the authors. We live in houses and breathe oxygen, just like you."

"Mmm…"

**** gives birth to the mechanical drive by chant, "this is Charlie's book, and this is Charlie. This is *****'s book, and this is *****. This is mine, I'm ****…"

"Tell them about the geniusfinger," I say. ***** nods and threatens to thumb-wrestle the next ten costumers.

One girl loosens an arm from an especially perplexed looking young man, and walks over to our booth. She spots ****'s book, *The Carney Years*.

"I've been to *Carney*!"

**** jumps up. "Here. Read the first page. It's free."

"Is that you on the cover?"

"No, I'm behind that tree."

The girl has an immediate fit of laughter and runs away. She does this five or six times, while ***** and I furtively retreat further and further away.

"He has this effect on women," I tell him.

I put on my best Han Solo gun belt, and light another cigarette.

. . . .

"I'm an English teacher," says the girl in the bar.

"Would like to take a look at it? I have a couple with me. I could *whip it out...*"

"That would be great. Sure."

I walk out the back door laughing, drunk, down a wooden wheelchair ramp, past the receding wall of the bar and by a large bald man who lives on a red stool looking at people suspiciously for a living.

I take a breath outside. No smoke. The air is cool. No eyes. I rescue a small briefcase, walk back into the bar, and hand the woman who claims to be an English teacher a small paperback book. She reads the back and laughs, tells me she will enjoy it, that her husband will be by in a moment to pay for it and would I like a beer?

"Yes. Thank you."

The woman tells me her friend is twenty seven. Close to my age. But she doesn't interest me.

I wander off.

. . . .

I am starting to notice the vague frequency in which little episodes come to pass like this—the meeting of an author I've held up as statue-worthy who ends up racing me to the bar rail and bumming cigarettes, or vice versa, or being the coal mine canary of independent deadbeat poets at a local small press convention, or reading an underlined passage from the dog-eared page of a book whose sales merely mean I'll have just enough gas money to keep the vicious cycle both vicious and cyclical. Every now and then, there is a phone call or an email asking me to mail fifteen signed copies of that awkward little paperback with my picture on the back jacket to Memphis for the book fair portion of the Elvis Pressley "A Perfect Day for Banana Sandwiches" convention, or three copies to a little shop in London that is in dire need of ashtrays. Or someone in a bar, or in the line at the post office asks what I do, and I tell them, and they give me fifteen dollars. I oblige, but very little of this seems too important, or more than a few molecules variant from the time before I was a mostly unheard of author, insignificant and invisible unless you asked, or unless there was a sign over my head pointed directly down at me.

Today, I feel like a neatly reluctant college student who has consented to take part in a vague medical experiment for ten dollars and a handful of sugar cookies and tomorrow I will probably feel a little luckier, or a little hungrier, or a little more orange than I do at this very moment in time. And that is all.

I am trying to make the most of my silly, confusing, uneven, erratic beast.

. . . .

I'm sitting in the passenger seat of Graham's rusty old station wagon. I've only just realized this. I wonder how long I've been here?

Tim is sitting in the back seat, trying to talk over the radio between fits of fiddling through empty packs of cigarettes. I think he's talking about girls, or the prospect of girls, or girls who used to have arms, or how long it's been since girls had arms. Or all four. Graham laughs in recognition from the very bottom stomach of his soul.

"I know. I know," he says. "I know, man. Dude, *I know!*"

I attempt to trace the outline of the horizon into the window.

Tim says he knows of a bar where arms have girls.

Graham muses about life in the city, and the shifting polarity of action and inaction, and all the bars that used to arm girls. Both of them talk as if they're not paying attention to each other so much as they are to the loose tie-ins of their own endlessly repeating inner choruses.

A man in a faded blue shirt takes five dollars away from us and sweeps our eyes toward a stage where someone far too old is singing a song that is far too young. A small crowd of people sway and order drinks.

Charlie Abrams swings her champion liver around a chipped pine-green bar rail. I watch her slow motion bar laugh consume all the smoke in the air. I watch the perfect, soft angle of her jawbone expand and contract. I watch her wide, twinkling lips dance.

She's talking to a wild-eyed redhead who seems to be doing a decent enough Mick Jagger impersonation. Graham flicks the light on.

I grab a beer.

Two pretty girls sit alone at the bar stirring up two glasses of pink water. The one on the left has a graceful, sort of Kate Beckinsale as an unreformed flapper thing going on. I watch the inevitable turnstile of pick-ups pass by, turn up the volume, and walk away with the unmistakeable look of crippled puppy failure.

I suddenly want to turn up the volume. Or contradict volume. Or say the word *volume* out loud.

"Tim—" I whisper.

"Yeah?"

"The two at the bar. Corner. Look at the One on the left with the short brown hair. White, button-up shirt."

"Oh, yeah. You going to say something?"

"*Volume.*"

Graham is talking to the redhead. Abrams is dancing on the pool table. Or maybe she's ordering a drink. I can't quite tell. She seems to be with several young men, most of which seem to be batting from the left.

One of them grabs me as I attempt to approach her arms; his eyes look like heavily caffeinated goldfish swimming behind bottle-thick black glasses.

"That's a great jacket," he sings. "Really, great. Where'd you get that? I can't believe someone would wear a jacket like that to *this* place."

"I, ah, always wear *this* jacket."

"It's a great jacket."

"I'll tell you what," I step back, "why don't you do me a big favor and tell all the lovely young women in this place what a great jacket I have on? I'll give you a nickel for each one."

The White Car pulls up in the middle of the bar, wearing a blue cotton chauffeur's hat cocked to one side—I can't tell which.

She's talking to someone. Now she's talking to someone else. Now someone is bringing her a beer. Now she's drinking it. Now, she's hitting the gas. I watch her signal left, and disappear into the other room. Her outline lingers in the center of my retinas the way light lingers in a bulb that's just burnt out.

Abrams pulls up a stool and signals the bartender. I run a red light, and ask her where the after-party is. She slurs something about her roommates being out of town, and how people are everywhere these days, and man—they should totally get beer.

I watch her and the redhead leave.

Graham sits next to me, nodding silently.

Tim curls his eyebrows at the band. "They're like a metaphor for everything that's wrong everywhere."

"Yeah..."

"The people are dancing. Make them stop dancing," his eyes say to no one in particular. "Is anyone starting anything?" he says to me in particular.

"I'll let you know."

"I'm ready for it."

Other people come and go. A painter, the once prettiest-girl-in-town-who-disappeared-months-ago appears right in front of me. Just like that.

Her eyes are perfect and her cheeks are perfect and her nose is perfect and her mouth, perfect, says things as if anyone needed ears at all, ever. I can't stand her face.

"You're a walking DaVinci."

"What?"

"Hello. Hi."

She gives me a hug, and tells me she'll be right back to talk.

"Send me a postcard!"

Abrams and the redhead reappear casually, dancing on tables, downing beers, and talking loudly to left-handed hitters.

Graham is rolling out a battle plan in his head. I can tell, because of the cartoon hourglass hovering over us. I imagine a hunter lying on his belly for weeks, calm, waiting for the exact right moment to buy a pack of endangered wolves a round of tequila shots.

"What are these girls doing later?" he asks, his voice like a Bond villian.

"They're having a party, I think."

"Awesome."

When the bar closes, the guys are kicked out and most of the girls allowed to linger. On the way out, I mention to Abrams and the redhead we might meet them at the house. They nod sort of mechanically.

Graham pulls around the corner and parks.

"Let's give them ten minutes." Everyone nods.

Ten minutes pass. I say we wait five more.

Tim starts scratching at the window. "What the fuck am I even doing here? There's no one here for me. Is anyone starting anything?"

"I'll let you know."

"I'm ready."

Five minutes pass. I write a note:

Maybe next time.

And leave it on the door with my phone number.

We drive down back roads and open several packs of cheap baseball cards. I stare at the trees passing, and wonder who they're waiting for. The passenger window always reminds me of elapsed-time footage. I imagine myself watching flowers bloom.

My phone is blinking.

"Hey Fell, where the hell are you?" Abrams rasps.

"Driving home. What are you doing?"

"Drinking! Why didn't you come by?"

"Ummm—I did. The note with the phone number you just dialed…"

"Oh, yeah. Right. Well, fuck, come on back, it's a party. We have beer.

Apparently, it comes in a can now!" she whispers.

"That's amazing…"

It really is. Oh, and Mick Jagger says bring whoever's with you."

"We'll be there." I hang up the phone and wait for the confetti.

Tim scratches at the door. "I think I'm just going to go. I don't feel like dancing."

Graham and I drop him off and drive backwards. There aren't any more trees, but I pretend not to notice. There's nothing on TV at this hour anyway.

Abrams's house is buzzing with people. The DaVinci is there, sitting on the kitchen counter with a young man who appears to have an insurmountable head start. We exchange nods.

There are others. There are total strangers, pacing, and a few waitresses from the bar. Everyone is drinking a beer and smoking a cigarette, and dancing on an imaginary table. Everything is loud, and everyone is naked; I am painting everyone naked.

The redhead is strikingly absent, and the overall ratio is well out of our favor. Graham and I decide to try and drink our way out.

We sit on the couch in the living room, exploring satellite radio. No one joins us, but eventually the house empties save for Abrams and a lone waitress who is affable but rather stout and plain, with very little to say to redeem her swollen, ordinary features.

We are recalled from outer space to play drinking games. I rob an orphaned pack of cigarettes from the table and watch Abrams sway around happily on ineffable 3 a.m. bar legs. Do I feel like dancing? I will have another beer and think about it.

Abrams throws a plastic ball into a plastic cup. I drink the contents, and enter myself in the dance competition. First prize is spinning nausea.

A half hour, or five minutes or three days later, we are all spread out on couches in the living room. I am sitting next to Abrams, and things are happening in elapsed time footage.

Graham smokes on the couch with the swollen waitress. He hopelessly explores the radio and starts to nod out.

We argue over stations. Eighties. Classic rock. Crap alternative. People are laughing at things I can't discern.

I try to make shapes out of the shifting backgrounds; the pale yellow square across the room is drifting off to the left and down, as if part of a falling star; it never hits the ground, but just keeps falling with the same objectiveless momentum.

I stumble, prehistorically, through the house to the bathroom and use the sink to make myself a glass of water. I try staring down the image in the mirror even though it won't stop shaking.

I'm sitting on the couch again. I'm losing time.

There's a head in my lap. I stroke its hair as the world slows down. All the shapes in the room slow down and dissipate. I close my eyes.

When I open them again I notice Graham sitting by himself. I lift the head off my lap and replace it gently on a pillow whose color I haven't yet decided upon.

"I'll be right back," I tell the head. It nods.

I fish my jacket out of the kitchen sink and give Graham my keys. He nods painfully, disappearing on ghost feet.

I kneel by the couch. "Do you want me to stay?"

The girl nods, leans backwards, and kisses me. Or I kiss her. Or we kiss each other. Her eyelashes are Van Gogh eyelashes. She opens her eyes between kisses, shuts them, smiles, and gets up to look around. There is no one.

"Do you want to go to bed?"

I nod.

The waitress is passed out on a couch in hallway leading to her room. We laugh a little, and creep by.

She turns out the lights.

And then she comes alive. Her eyes, now open cat-wide, drill unrepairable holes in me. She seems determined. She grins. I kiss away the grin.

I feel like a child in space. I am weightless, and am thinking of asking her why the sky is suddenly so blue.

My right hand brushes strands of dark brown hair away from her face. I kiss away the growing smirk, and we disappear into darkness.

. . . .

A few hours later, I open my eyes and attempt to circle the bizarre blurry planet I've landed on.

I trace the warm curves of the naked body laying dead beside me. Her arches ache in all best ways possible. Her inverted spine and the bed are making a tourniquet on my left arm, but I don't care. My legs are stiff from lying tangled and bloodless in hers, but I don't care. My neck is going to crack for days when I get up, but I don't care.

A little white cat jumps up onto the base of the bed and purrs at my big toe. I agree with it.

There's a girl passed out in the next room, and the door isn't all the way closed. I know she's still there because I'm noticing things; it's one of those sliding doors that closes into the wall, only, it doesn't close all the way; there's no latch.

That door has probably never had the experience of being closed. Even last night, while we spun webs and she asked if I were a certain drum-beating pink rabbit. Even while she moaned, and took a chunk out of my right arm and begged me to keep going. The bruise will probably be there for days, but I don't care.

I'm memorizing the walls. The clock turns over. 9:33. 10:15. 10:42. 11:24.

Sometimes she stretches, and I move my hand over her stomach and she purrs. Sometimes she pulls my fingers together with hers as if they belonged to

145

her. My fingers are stiff and bloodless, but I don't care.

Her right shoulder smells like the echo of a flower shop; it has a thin, sweet smell. Just there; just enough.

Sometimes her head spins, and she kisses me with her eyes closed, and smiles and falls backwards.

I am memorizing everything so later, when I am nowhere, when I am all alone with stale, borrowed indoor air, or spring shivers, or Tim talking about museums full of arms, I have something.

Purring. Sixes. Maybe Lilac. Great eyelashes. Sliding stomach. Likes my hands. Legs making homemade bracelet twists. A kitchen with a small stove. Doesn't snore. Smiles with her eyes closed. Cat name—

Cat name. Cat name. Cat name. California roll? Eggplant? Larry? Sam? Apple? Peter? Parker? Peaches? Patches? Paul? George? Ringo? Dostoyevsky?

Things make noises, but no one moves. My eyelids hurt, but I don't care. I have something.

I have the smoke in my lungs. I have her hair in my eyelashes. I have all my skin, and all her skin, and awful bar-beer-cigarette-death morning sickness and stiff joints, and center-of-the-earth warmth, and a thin blanket that's slowly disappearing, and a poor nameless cat.

I think of Audrey Hepburn singing on her little Manhattan fire escape. I think of my favorite window in New York City. I think of disappearing orange globes catching fire. I think of the vampire sunlight I'll have to face later and I don't care.

146

I have something for later. I've learned to store such things.

. . . .

I take pictures on the drive home. I photograph the faces I pass in the passing windows of passing cars. I invent stories based on their posture, and what's hanging from their rear view mirror.

Ruth, 63, is a crossing guard who used to be a housewife. Her husband died six years ago, and left her next to nothing. They never had any children, and weren't very religious. In the evening she listens to the radio to pass the time.

Emmings, 47, is an insurance claims adjuster. On weekends, he sells model trains at a flea market just over the Delaware state line. When he was five, he and his second cousin Wally played doctor while his parents were out shopping. He never told anyone. Sometimes he watches baseball and cries.

I light a cigarette and hold it up over the sun with my right hand. The smoke feels like sand against my throat.

. . . .

A few nights later I see Abrams and the redhead at the same bar. We are business-like, which is to say we are awful.

"Hey Fell."

"Hey Abrams. Drinking?"

"Usually…"

I feel like I should shake her hand and tell her to "keep up the good work." But there's a band playing behind us, and some of the people are dancing.

. . . .

Once there was a pressing odyssey. Then there was a release.

For a long time, things went like this. Gravity went down and we all woke up, wondering about truth and questioning answers in constant contradictory pressing and releasing minds.

Man loves us a triangle and a saucer shape. Woman, the opposite. Connect four, and carve up a park bench in minimalist acronym haiku; twelfth anniversary, and skywriting.

How can anyone tell the difference?

"I saw your name the other day."

"Cumulous?"

"Orange, and evaporating. Maybe it was just your eyes closing against mine."

I see the same monochrome test-pattern each time I close my eyes. I cum twenty one grams every time. I marry the shapes running through my head to the tips of my fingers. I claw my way through each series of blinks, waiting for the dam to break when we can all swim into pink triangular heaven together.

Whoever is on top is always taller. Gravity carries your breath to all the places your fingers forget. Do you remember my breath? Will I remember yours in another day?

Once upon a time, all the hair on my head actually opened up, and I saw stars. Galaxies of stars.

Henry and I walk around the yard. It's almost raining; the world is thinking about raining. The world looks as if it's just had six Big Gulps on a long, stopless car trip.

We throw a football through the air and it catches the imagination of rain, and slips through our fingers. Sometimes it's weighed down by sheer atmosphere. A little dog imagines herself chasing a football, but decides against it.

Henry pauses for a cigarette. I watch him, and imagine myself having one. I write a play in my head on how I'd ask him for one:

"Henry?"

"What?"

"Can I get a cigarette, man?"

"Bitch."

Scene.

I scan the horizon sans cigarette. The house is behind us. In front, and to the left, are wide expanses of field broken a hundred yards or so away by trees and small, one-story houses. The fields are shallow, the color of milk-watered coffee. In the fall there'll be corn. I think. I think I remember there being corn in the fall. Or, maybe it was just a meaningless spurt of grass? Or maybe it was last March? Maybe there was a background revolt that we were unaware of, and I only assumed corn.

I, cigaretteless, watch the sun take a dive. It occurs to me that there has never been a bad sunset anywhere. Ever. Occasionally, the sun invents new shades of red or yellow or an eerie off-blue or a combination of all three, but every single shade of fire it invents is lovely. I imagine the first time someone saw fire they stared at the colors for days before they realized it was warm, useful, or destructive. I imagine those first moments were spent in rabid fascination of pure color, and the way things dance.

Henry decides we need a new game. We think for a while. We scan the surroundings. There's a rusted metal trashcan by the house where we send things to die.

Once, we had a pet rooster who wandered into the yard. We named him Colonel Sanders, and fed him chicken-flavored oodles of noodles, thinking ourselves hilarious. One night I spent twenty minutes trying to get him to come into the porch out of the rain. He looked so pathetic in the rain. He looked like a depressed lizard in a wet cat suit.

A few weeks later he discovered a new smell. Colonel had something black on his back. We imagined it was manure from the nearby farms he wandered off to, or from. A few days later, he died, horribly, on our sidewalk, and by the following day he was almost completely decomposed. Henry took a pitchfork and spooned the decayed remains into the rusted metal trashcan. I poured the gasoline, and Henry lit the match. We did the same thing with a turtle once, who we found frozen in the driveway. More than a few times we played tennis with a loaded mousetrap.

Henry picks up a twelve-foot solid shaft of a tree, and decides we're going to have a throwing contest. We agree on a starting line, stand back, run to it, and hurl the shaft with our palms cradled together under it. When we get bored of this we decide instead to joust the trashcan crypt.

A white car pulls up and something walks out of it, and I suddenly don't want to be jousting trashcan crypts.

"What are you guy *doing*?"

Henry explains what we are doing. The girl opens her mouth like a surprised cartoon, and stands perfectly still for a while. I aim the wooden shaft for the opening. I run at full speed, and connect with perfect accuracy. Henry laughs until he doesn't.

I can stand perfectly still. I can do this for hours without blinking.

The girl puts her teeth back in her cartoon mouth and goes inside. And then it finally starts to rain.

. . . .

I drive to the city to see Claire, and to do another in an endless series of readings which don't sell books, but do charge my credit card for the exact amount of beer it takes to get me on a stage in front of real, live human beings.

"Hi. I'm Charlie, and I'm a recovering author," I say to mixed laughter and awkward silence. My hands break into a warm, sticky sweat as I thumb open a small paperback.

Henry David Thoreau's grandson's fourth cousin twice removed and thrice imprisoned used to be one of Bill's roommates in college. One night—after an unusually productive chemistry class—Bill and he were standing on the porch when HDT vanished suddenly. Bill looked around for a moment before realizing his inebriated friend had collapsed at his feet, falling facefirst onto his beer bottle and shattering it underneath him.

"I ffthink I fffell," he said, dreamily.

"You okay?" Bill asked.

"Fffine, Fffine," he said, pulling himself up. Bill tried to help him inside, but was brushed off as HDT stumbled into the kitchen, tucking a pair of fresh beers into his pockets, and crawling up the stairs on his belly like a pale, handicapped slug. Three minutes later, Bill swore he could hear HDT rumbling back down the stairs, followed by the sharp squeak of the fridge reopening.

Bill tiptoed into the hallway, and watched as his friend crawled back up on his belly and squirmed toward his bed, tripping over a nearby TV stand, and sending the innocent TV over the stairwell, dangling awkwardly by its thin, black umbilical chord.

"You okay up there, buddy?" Bill called out.

"Whateryou, my fffucking fffather?" HDT answered.

In the morning, Bill and his other roommate, Vic, found HDT's bloated body laying facedown in the kitchen, pants around his ankles, wrapped around the fridge, and snoring like a broken jet engine.

"Do you want to shave his head or can I?" Vic asked.

"Let's take turns," Bill said.

"That was great," Claire assures me.

"Can we go now?"

She nods.

Back at her house, I pull a bottle of whiskey out of the freezer and put it out of its misery. Claire winks at me. I turn on the television as she slips away into her bedroom to sleep.

. . . .

What am I filled with? It doesn't feel like blood. It doesn't feel like anything human.

It doesn't even feel like matter—it feels like a force. It feels like an asteroid's exact moment of impact. It feels like everything is about to come apart at once. The transition can't be soft, or rhythmic; it has to be violent. It all feels so very violent. All my organs want to go off in different directions, and my heart is beating on the wall again, and all I want to do is sleep.

"You're all spies," I mutter again, and again.

I haven't had a drink. I haven't gone fishing. I haven't been the ninth caller and won the weekend pass. I haven't fallen for anything. I'm just combusting. I'm coming apart. I don't know how to stop. I don't even know if I care enough to stop.

I'd like to sleep, but I'm not so excited about the waking up part. I have no expectations of the morning. I should go to the post office. I should eat something. I should get some air. I should take someone else's vitamins. I should move something a little to the left. Even a few inches.

I ought to just start running. I ought to shave all my hair off. I ought to want to change the light bulbs. There's nothing that's not combustible right now. I don't care what I've got sitting in the back of the refrigerator, and I don't care who the Orioles are playing. I don't care about the drink specials. I don't care about the electric bill. I don't care about the whales, or that children in Africa are starving. I'm drifting. I've constructed this whole contrary existence around the possibility of drifting and now I'm bitching about the raft.

I want something, I can tell you that, but I don't believe in the things I want anymore. It's like wanting dragons, or the goddamned tooth fairy. Yes, that's it. I want a fucking quarter under my pillow. Is that too much to ask? If I stop breathing for lack of quarters, will the world be any different?

For as long as I can remember, all my friends have attempted to fight off my crazy by telling me what a great, wonderful, genius human being I am. They could tell me I won the goddamned lottery while curing AIDS and saving kittens from burning mosques for all I fucking care. They could tell me my cock made People Magazine's fifty most beautiful list. They could stuff my left arm and serve it for Christmas dinner. Maybe then I'd get a decent tan. Maybe then all the throbbing would stop. Maybe all I need is a good stuffing.

Yes, that's it. I want a girl that glows in the dark, and doesn't mind having her skin sanded down to an idea—to the cave painting formula for form—to the unsteady perfect sound of an emotion. I want everything boiled down to its most simplistic, pure, spotless essence. Is that too much to ask?

I want complete apolitical liberty, and I want total control of all of it. If I wake up offended by the weather, I want the very idea of weather revoked. If the sky is the wrong color, I want to be able to change the channel. I want to be able to talk to strangers the way roses talk to seasoned, perfect lovers. I want someone to kiss my earlobe, and tell me I'm not sixty-five percent water. I want to crawl inside the very chalk outline of woman. I want to stop breathing oxygen, and start breathing skin.

I want all knowledge of science gone. I want complete mystery. I want the sun stapled shut. I want to rewrite the purpose of every human body part.

I want to forget God. I want to stop feeling like God has forgotten me. I want God to get the hell out of my alphabet soup.

I want a car air freshener that smells like an autumn sweater. I don't want anyone to worry about me when I crawl home at night. In fact, I want to be carried home on the world's fingertips, and I want to be able to make the world dance ridiculous campfire tribal dances so absurd and pure and unrestricted that their very ideas were previously only imagined on massive acid trips by people in comas. I want madness and liberation to be understood as the same thing, and I want nothing else understood. I want desire to roll off like cigarette ash in the wind. I want peace. I want deathpeace. I want lovepeace. I want sexpeace. I want sleeppeace. I want to combine the sensations of drunkenness, orgasm, victory and thanksgiving dinner overdose. I want to take the blue pill. Someone give me the fucking blue pill. I'm serious.

155

I want to unravel the insides of all the violent electricity of the human mind and set it loose. I'm giving up this form. I want to boil down all the truth in the universe, so I can stuff it in my mouth and grind my teeth over it. Is that too much to ask?

All I ever wanted to be was smiling light bulb wire.

Tomorrow I will buy a gun. Tomorrow I will go to the bank. Tomorrow I will write the teller a note demanding I be given the blue pill. This is serious. If the lid doesn't come off the revolution soon, there's going to be real trouble.

All I want is a little revolution. All I want is to unravel time and matter and meaning. Is that too much? The world feels like a song with no beginning and no end, and the middle never stops skipping. All I want is a clean second without so much skipping. All I want is a little sleep. Is that too much?

Give me the blue pill, teller. No one's looking. Pull down your socks and let's go dancing.

. . . .

I wake up with the foggy recollection of a handful of small, multicolored pills and a crowd of blurry faces. My tongue tastes like paint thinner, my stomach kicks, and I fall directly into a shivering, uneasy nausea.

"Hello consequence."

"Hello, Charlie. How long has it been?"

"Hours."

My eyes crack on the lights in the bathroom, and everything splinters into hard white rain. Thirteen years of bad lungs pour out into the heel end of my left shoe. I pull the laces over my head and make a noose.

A dam somewhere inside my stomach breaks, and I make pretty greenish-yellow clouds inside the toilet bowl. They swirl around for a few minutes before congealing into an island.

I manage to make it to the car without vomiting again. The air smells like spoiled double cheeseburgers and ghost-smoke. I pour hot glue into my nostrils.

Two and a half hours later, I turn down Pennsylvania Avenue, mistaking it for West Chase Street and something under me explodes. I pull over to pronounce my front driver's side tire officially dead. I am pretending to breathe, and the sky is pretending not to rain. And the Academy Award goes to…

The jack behind the seat is broken. I am staring down a street that curves, almost straight downward, into an increasingly dark field of shattered glass and row houses. I look around for a phone booth or a hang glider.

It starts raining even harder. I wave to all the nice policemen who drive by, but don't dare stop to help.

The greenish-yellow mass in my stomach pulses against the blowing storm. I can feel it rushing to greet me. I bend over and make another island.

There's a pay phone across the street. I make a run for it. Or, rather, I make a calculated fall for it.

The phone doesn't seem to have any powers of communication, but it does magically change all my quarters into nickels. I kick it a couple times, and no one seems to mind. I cut my hand on its throat.

Then it starts to pour actual kittens.

A young black kid in wet bum clothes asks if I need a hand. Bleeding, covered in grime and glowing green, I happily accept. He hails the next car that passes by and negotiates a jack from the driver for the princely sum of four dollars.

He works the jack while I tear off the lug nuts. After we're finished I buy the jack, give him a couple of dollars and a ride through a few miles of shattered glass.

Forty-five minutes later, I find the shop where I'm supposed to be reading, and walk in with my right hand wrapped in a bloody t-shirt and rest of me soaked in cloudburst and oil.

**** greets me, hands me a cheese sandwich and a beer, and tells me we're opening for some sort of "poetry slam."

He doesn't ask any questions.

We read.

I get the usual laughs for my Gerald Ford as Hunter Thompson impressions, and some people actually buy our books for a change, and everything is suddenly all very lovely.

Then the owners talk us into judging the slam.

**** and I order two beers each and proceed to listen to ninety minutes of Marilyn Manson lyrics and middle school raps about expensive shoes and terribly shiny rhyming dictionaries, and I can only assume its all meant to be very deep and personal.

**** winces. I nod, and we give everyone sixes.

"We're the Russian judges," I insist over the chorus of boos.

"We're arrogant assholes," **** mutters.

"Who are published…"

We wink, and clink glasses.

158

I down four more beers, get vague directions, and walk back into the storm to attempt the trek home.

I turn left.

Two blocks later, I am pulled over by a loud flash of violet lights. A woman in a blue suit tells me I have a loose tire cord. I tell her I didn't know. She asks to see my owner's manual, fixes the cord while I stumble behind her and gives me better directions.

I get in the car and turn up the stereo, as the four leaf clover on my dashboard bursts into flames.

. . . .

I wake up at six thirty the next morning wondering if I am going to be sick, wondering if I should just get it over with and check myself into a hospital and have them check for everything they can check for. Maybe they'll finally give me the blue pill.

What does it mean? What does it all want? I desperately want to collar this tiresome melancholy away and haul it straight back to the awful mystical depths from whence it came. If I could only find the light switch. How do people do such things?

I am staring at the ceiling. I am trying not to stare at the ceiling. I'd try sealing the stairs if I had any.

I am lost in the possibility of blue lights, of wondering what possibilities are even possible, worthwhile, affordable, or what kind of money back guarantee I can get for even imagining thinking about the possibility of considering the idea of wondering about the prospect of goodness in this world.

Half of me wants to disappear altogether, like a handful of sand thrown into the wind. Half of me wants some real, honest manner of crushing goodness to tend to. Three quarters of me wants another cheese sandwich.

I have all these odd devils on my shoulder: Youth. Sex. Time. Money. Knowledge. Talent. Desire. Friendship. Facility. Family. Faustism. Freedom. Cheddar. Mozzarella. Gouda.

I don't know where to turn, but around, around, around—

. . . .

Eddie pulls up and idles in the driveway. We exchange wild aeronautical hand gestures.

"You look like shit," he says.

"Costume party."

"You win?"

"Nobody wins, Eddie."

I'm laughing again, and again I don't know why.

"Quit thinking about it and get dressed."

"How do you do that?"

"Black people thing. You took us out of our homeland and enslaved us, so now we can all read your minds."

"That sounds fair."

"It ain't thirty acres and a mule, but what the fuck? Now get dressed white devil."

"Where're we going?"

"Pizza Hut to meet Carter and steal a credit card, Rent-a-Car to grab a 15-passenger van, Terry's to open a pack of baseball cards, mall to see a free movie and pick up a few people, out to the bar then some girl's hotel room, and the free clinic in the morning. We'll have you home by August."

"I've gotta be home by seven."

160

"Naw, you're coming with us tonight."

"Can't Eddie…"

"What the fuck have you got to do?"

"The girls are coming over and…"

"What girls?"

"Eve and Piera. They left a note…"

"Don't you know any girls with normal names?"

"No…"

"That it? That's all?"

"Well, they're bringing booze. Look, it's all in the note. Beautiful handwriting…"

"So you're going to throw away a barful of possibilities for two cold-shouldered women who won't sleep with you and a couple sixes of free beer?"

"Hell yeah!"

"I can't let you do that Charlie. You're coming with us and that's final."

"Eddie…"

"Come on, it's gonna be one of the last trips."

"What're you doing the rest of the week?"

"Moving."

"Oh, yeah. Shit…"

"You're coming with us."

"Some other time, man. Not tonight. Now let it go before I beat you over the head with your fucking broken car handle."

"See, that was unnecessary. Why do you have to bring violence in everything?"

"I'm sorry…"

"I should kick your scrawny white ass for that shit. Come on. Get in the goddamned car before you make me pretend to be mad."

Carter isn't at Pizza Hut.

We find him on the front porch of a four-story dust mansion that looks like it might be centuries old. Huge, stained-glass windows look like pearls inside oysters. A large white electric bell hangs over the arches of the main doorway. Armies of intricate grey cobwebs dance over the railing, and several sizable animal sculptures fan the lawn. I wonder if I've stumbled into a John Waters movie.

Next to Carter is a girl I took out once, confused deeply, and never called back. Behind them, a wiry little kid with long stringy comic book convention hair and wire-rimmed glasses paces back and forth, talking excitedly to a large, older woman who might be his mother.

Inside the house, there are an innumerable amount of flaccid wooden stairwells, old pianos, wide screen digital televisions, semi-pregnant-looking cats, skeletal wooden ceiling fans, and two pairs of moderately overweight but jolly sisters who seem to be getting ready for a grade-school play, but are probably more truthfully getting ready for a fragrant failure at a local bar.

Eddie floats around like a hummingbird peaking on Adderall. He steals cigarettes from Carter, pretends to throw the wiry kid over the porch, helps the old woman hang a copper fish over one of the windows, bruises the girl I took out once on the left arm, tries to set me up with one of the overweight sisters, sells seventeen tickets to the moon, and manages to get all the words to my least favorite U2 song completely wrong.

But after a half hour, he convinces one of the girls to loan him a credit card for the van rental, and we pull off to open a pack of baseball cards along a back road on the way to the movies.

I only manage to score a few relief pitchers and the starting second baseman for the Mets, but still manage to consume a $628 tub of popcorn and a forty-seven liter pitcher of Coke.

Back at the house, Jude, Tim, James Watson, and a few other people without names sit in odd pagan circles around several large mounds of Wendy's cheeseburgers. Eddie wanders back and forth on a cell phone headset, shouting and waving his arms like he's on the verge of selling capitalism to the Chinese. When he finally hangs up, I congratulate him, hold a press conference, and watch him disappear into the night and clubland.

Eve and Piera show up shortly after, carrying several bottles of juice, a liter and a half of rum, and a large bag of crushed ice. I make for a butter knife to butcher the melting mound into cubes, while Eve settles in and Piera opens an air conditioner shop on the couch.

Piera Bella is a pretty-as-hell 22-year-old with giant brown eyes that suck all the neighboring light around her into their spacey gleam. She also has a razor-sharp wit that's only slightly hampered by the painfully slow deliberation of her speech patterns. Currently, the New York Post is reporting that she's into Watson. Watson meanwhile is into a faceless pharmacist from the city who is apparently not so much into her boyfriend.

I, on the other hand, am into hammering away at my liver and doing my very best at avoiding forcing the moment to its crisis.

I am into walking to the fridge to get another.

"I won't even tell you about that," Watson assures a small crowd in the kitchen. "All I can say is, it had something to do with the rear end."

"I think you just gave it away…"

"Is this the story about the…"

"…asshole fissure…"

"I mean, there are already two perfectly good openings, why…"

"What's a fissure?"

"It's like a canyon. A ravine."

Tim starts laughing wildly.

"No it's not, it's more like a tear. A *torn* asshole."

"…broken anal cavity…"

Bright, sweepingly recalcitrant laughter mixes with all the damp cigarette smoke and dry fan air. I walk out backwards, more than a little afraid.

I sit down on a toadstool, and tell Piera that I breathe oxygen too.

"Just like you!"

She rolls her eyes at me and stares longingly at the DVD player.

Somewhere between conversations about maple syrup and my own obsessive desperations of tongue parachutes, the sky breaks and billions of bright raindrops dive-bomb the burnt summer earth outside. Consequently, Watson and I decide it's a good time to play football.

I wonder if the government will later report that we were only playing with a weather balloon as Watson's first throw hits me in the chest. I am laughing again, and I finally know why.

The rain makes everything blurry, just like the booze, but the rain doesn't hate you in the morning. The rain doesn't re-imagine you as hyper-ephemeral

164

lovers or front page news stories. The rain doesn't give you courage and it doesn't take away your internal organs. It just falls—it falls and shatters and dissipates, and rises and falls again.

Back inside, Jude, Tim, and the others with and without names disappear into the dull blank void of Monday night nothingness. Watson and I fall onto the living room floor grasping for air, and accidentally dry ourselves off with what turns out to be Henry's test-pattern bathrobe.

"That touched his nuts man," Watson points out unhappily.

Time passes and bottles roll, and Eve becomes her usual narcoleptic self, and Piera becomes her usual quiet icecap, and I my usual despondent poor man's Citizen Kane, and only Watson is left to urge on the music playing in the background.

"This is Coltrane?"

"This and the last twenty-two minutes."

When we open a pack of baseball cards, Piera sits dully on the edge of my bed staring off into the darkest recesses of space, or dreamy-eyed at Watson, or, occasionally, sort of like a confused, out of focus Labrador at me. And into the night we all disappear together—rising and falling and dissipating and shattering into seemingly endless pieces, only to wake up in the morning again having barely moved at all.

. . . .

There's a kitchen knife stuck in the grey mat message board in the middle of my wall. It's holding up an L-shaped manifestly faded piece of newspaper that's about to turn to ash.

I want to go somewhere, and do something like meet a goldfish or buy something with two legs a drink, or invent the single cigarette vending machine, but I don't. I don't like to drive. I don't really enjoy crowds. I don't like being able to discern between the voices in the great hum, because no one really talks about anything but talking about things, and getting fucked up while doing things, and precluding to things that will never come close to actually happening. Everyone says, "I got so fucked up yesterday..." or "oh my god, (insert predicate)!"

Half of me wants to fall at once madly in love with everything around me, and half of me refuses on the grounds that people have eyes and senses and that these things all lead to discrimination, which is natural, but evil, which is also natural, of which I've grown tired and am hereby protesting gravity and the avoidance of white after labor day. And, I'm not even dwelling on the everyday color, shape, wallet, or wear discriminations—I'm dwelling on the discrimination of the one thing that's worse than ignorance, and that's fear. No one writes editorials, or forms political action committees or charitable foundations on people who discriminate against basic human breathing patterns, and this is why I abhor the whole entirety of humanity as a basic principal— because we're are all blind, because I am defending myself, and because there is an overall instinctively negative reaction to fear in this terrified world.

Dogs smell fear and become aggressive. Women smell fear and become lawyers. Lawyers smell fear and become dogs. It's a vicious cycle! I'm afraid of sunlight, I can't talk to strangers, my looks lay land mines, and I don't wear enough bright colors. So what if I breathe 60% more nitrogen than the leading brand? So what if I walk fast? So what I have duct-taped the insides of my right sleeve together, or that it doesn't tell you what I'm thinking on the back of my car? So what if I'm rubbing all the blood out of my bottom lip, and I only really dyed my hair so you'd forget what I look like? So what if there's still gravity? Who cares if there's a movie playing somewhere and you're not in it? Go, run! Catch it! Be in all the movies! I don't care anymore! Take me off the list and never call again!

I will not respond. I will not be the ninth caller. I don't want your tickets, and I'm not sending flowers ever again. So what if I'm holding the neck of this bottle? I've pressurized the exterior, and I'm hinting at steam, so what if my wishes don't always end in complete sentences?

So what if I'm not batting my eyelashes at the moment? I'm so fucking tired. Go ahead and count the rings on my forehead. Count the dark circles on each side of my fucking nose. I didn't stay awake all night because I was waiting for the sunset, or working towards making unripe peaches scream—I stayed awake all night because I couldn't turn the volume on my own heartbeat down low enough to concentrate anymore.

And this is the fucking honest truth. Is this better? Fuckoff, I'm tired. I wanted to say something timeless about your eyes, but really, there's a reason there's a knife in the grey mat message board in the middle of my wall.

I'm putting an end to discrimination right now. I'm cutting off all my senses and mailing them to the Van Gogh museum. But I don't want a receipt. Or a tracking number. I want another fucking shot. I want another multicolored pill. I want to earn the disorientation I've been feeling for the past twenty-five years. I want to earn all the space between us. I want to light this individually wrapped cigarette on your cold shoulder. I want to learn how to make thirty minute brownies in twenty minutes.

I consider taking out a personal ad:

Dear America: I want to get laid. Look at what a nice guy I am! I look at walls and remember things. I will write about our exploits later, and I will leave out all the shit about being drunk and the last people in the bar. I just enjoy a nice warm body. A nice, young, well-shaped, female body. Look how deep I am. I have pretty blue eyes and dark hair. I'm so pretty. And deep. So fucking deep.

Smoke, as a rule, naturally curls into a pair of dim circles and lingers in front of me at will. I stare through it. I have another. I listen to everything burning.

Inside my house, the tiles on the floor clap, and everything smells like it came in a bag from the Sharper Image. And every atom in my body is volcanic. And I can't move; I am somehow able to simultaneously stand perfectly still and shiver apart. I'm picking up signals from ghosts. They want grief and destruction in no particular order.

patter. patter. patter. click. whir. wire.

Foremost, we must discard the davenport immediately and jettison the ashtrays. Upstreet, left, hang one for the team and lean in for old time, and the river run run run hey hey sssrrrrrrrrrr...n o p a u s e...straight into the well, Timmy, and tell the fires to keep it coming! By morning, no one'll notice all the flowerbeds are empty and we're all still upkeep atop the clothesline spinning our faces in fragile mirrors, brown, a little green, a mood ring, closed, open, closed, flytrap. Full of ink when not looking.

I'm singing to this streetlight, and there's nothing you can do about it. A thousand things tell me to sing. I look across the lawn and forget what I see almost immediately. On a regular basis, I look up and imagine what never existed.

I turn around when the rain tells me too. My shoulders are all wet. I watch the phone, half in the ground, a sad flower, and become swallowed and tongueless. And I understand tonguelessness.

> *"man, this is no mere abject corollary—"*
> *people say things like these and like to wear ties*
> *on the back stove, waiting*
> *collar yer own omen*
> *bed tooth sleep tonight,*
> *or short the orderly a nice sign*
> *ashpants for ashplants, we all fawn down.*

Were there a bed for the scraping, I would take her and straw out her very marrow this very minute. Menthol, or not, I know how to swim on blacksheets. Breathing. Always breathing. And always pausing

169

and telling us not to pause. Never pause. Rage. Urge. Circle. Spell the alphabet on all her pink parts. Prepare for boarding. I'll be the captain. Starboard!

In a clean and distinct drawl, walking out into the street to admire something I meant to half forget to call tomorrow at six. Or seven. Yes, seven is late enough. Seven will sound ordinary. Everyone likes ordinary. Ordinary sevens.

Passing through it all, I feel somewhat cheated. Where're all the bodies? This gaunt won't let that one go, and yet, we're all still wearing shoes and talking about the Clash even though they're gone. Dead. I'd like to find that ironic. Do I? Would they?

Passing through the passing throughs, we're all intermittent, I s'pose.

Everything. I wish everything would pick up and pass current, and there'd always be some nice electricity to ignore. Some mock reaction. Some religious foreplay. Sneak up and tickle a priest's asshole and see if he yells "GOD."

The pills I took are working. Don't tell anyone, we're almost there. Over by the driveway, there's something on wheels, and around the corner is another series of things we've just simply got to destroy. Meet me in the tree house in a half hour, I've got to find a better hat.

The world wishes it could curl up into this—this size, this heat. This slow drift about the near-electric

170

humming of skin. Tin soldiers and Nixon's tracing the delicate destruction, the tenderized blue marks, the ailing joints, the pools on our backs and chests. The fingerprints left behind all the stories. Tracing the last bruised clutches of that last moment that must've been like heaven without cable, which is to say, heaven.

Through cans, eyes, things that don't matter, things that want to matter, mere matter, near matters, all fool crisis and all flakes of skin and hope abandoned, I am rendered, as all of you, eventually, feeling little more than slight and abandoned flakes of time itself. No matter draw matter between this or that or a breath or a can of spray paint, or an erudite eradication of something desperately human, or the wrong eyeliner, or fine wine with fish—

I have.........figured it out—cleverness proceeds essence. Existence be damned. Paper, rock, scissors, dirty bomb.

All matter of pretending its' mattering is the great desert mirage we've all read, heard, polished, and soiled about. This suit and that haircut, and that lapel pin and that degree, and that barwit and those shoes, that steadiness—this all eliminates the humanity I foolishly imagined, or penned, or spray painted. I forgot! I forgot about boats and rides, tides, flashes and ephemera, and was too wrapped up in mere reporting!

I regret to inform you that I will be leaving my position, as it were.

171

Yours most truly—

-charlie fell

. . . .

VII. Ladies and Gentlemen, We are Floating in Space.

There's a forest between us—between all of us—and the shade is simply killing me.

Some time ago, someone stole all my socks and now I've forgotten how to move altogether. I've forgotten, even, how to get dressed, or why, or what *is* the capital of Paraguay?

Last night I watched someone walking into things which weren't there, but surely happened, which later won't have happened, but will then happen again. But then again none of this is really happening at all. Film at eleven.

I am bored with repetition. I'm bored with people who are constantly being rewarded for cleverness disguised as repetition. I'm bored with people who sit in circles, pretending things are important.

I'm tired of feeling like some important bag of wheat. I'm bored with the answers. Moreover, I don't believe in them. Moreover, if there were any *real* answers, I still wouldn't have the right questions.

I'm bored with the track-loop of social action. I am bored with the politics of breathing. I want to be paint on a ceiling fan. I want out, but I'm bored with the notion of wanting out.

Do I contradict myself? I'm hungry and probably have liver damage. It is large, and contains multitudes.

I'm tired of statues that don't have arms.

The ceiling fan has stopped spinning. Sometimes, I wonder about apples.

apples. apples. apples.

I am saying things. "Apples."

I wonder why the air has to be so much ash. I wonder why I collect air. I wonder about eyelids.

If I close my eyes tight enough, I can see inside everyone's eyelids. They all hover in vertical patterns, like a wallpaper made of memory. The insides are all the same color, always magenta or burgundy, or whatever color tissue and blood make when held up to a light. Everything is glowing and so painfully beautiful, I can't stand it. I wonder if I can clench my jaw tight enough to taste the salt inside of everyone's pupils?

Today, I woke up and my eyelids were on the fourth floor, and I was in the lobby.

I am going to complain to the manager, lipless.

. . . .

I open a pack of limited-edition hologram cards, and for the next half hour I think about doing things.

I want to do things. I really do. It's just that my skin won't stop vibrating.

I am enjoying my skin vibrating.

Two dogs aim at death and couches, running circles, chewing, lapping, tossing, yelping, wincing, falling, like some bizarre sex act—like foreplay. Like foreplay on a bottle of cough syrup—like the world is melting away and there is nothing else to do but chew it up and dance.

The world is a brown blur of animal dances.

I want to find a girl right this minute, right now with my skin vibrating, and I want to chew up a couch.

Or dinner. Yes, maybe dinner would be better first. Maybe salad and breadsticks should precede a mouthful of toilet paper.

Maybe I should tell someone my skin is vibrating?

Suddenly, all the colors in the world look the same. Only, I don't know this for sure, because everything is blue.

Also, I seem to be moving a little more—slowly now than normal. Things around me dart and flash, but I don't mind. In fact, it would take something quite disturbing to make me want to get up from this chair I've fallen into. Only, I'm not going to think about such things, because my skin is vibrating and everything is blue and flashing.

I hear things off in the distance and I want to go to them—I want to see what the hearing things are. I want a better vocabulatory power over the descriptive indescribability of things. My awareness of the English language, and my ability to explain myself as anything more than a semi-rational houseplant, seem somewhat hindered.

The President is on television saying things. I think he's stuttering a little, but I'm not sure. That is, I cannot say for sure because my skin is vibrating, and everything is blue, and flashing, and my awareness of the English language, and my ability to explain myself with any real sort of vocabulatory power is somewhat hindered.

One of the dogs is walking by me. The black one. I can tell that he's breathing. I can tell, because his breath is sitting on my elbow and waving at all the little hairs on my arm. It appears that I am able to collect such things—things such as breath.

Two children are arguing. I think it's on television, but I don't think the president is still on. And I don't really care, because I'm collecting breath.

I wish I had more breath to collect. I wish I could wall myself up in a roomful of expelling lungs. I wish I could watch the diaphanous expansion of life in real time, life size, and broadcast on the insides of my eyelids. I wish I could curl up in a warm breeze of carbon dioxide. I wonder how long it would take to me to choke and die in diaphanous carbon dioxide eyelid heaven?

It occurs to me that everyone dies eventually. This does not rattle my brain too much, because I've been to college and know all about pretentious bullshit baseball card revelations. I even got an A on the final.

Now I am shivering a little, because my breath is gone. I wonder where it's gone, but I don't wonder too long, because I've been to college.

Someone else is on television now. He has on a flannel shirt, and is sitting down and frowning. I'm not frowning. My mouth is open, and I am breathing. I take a deep breath and feel my skin quietly stretch across my bones. Maybe I should eat more? I am getting a little light lately. I wonder if this has anything to do with college?

I wonder if women like skinny twenty-something authors who collect breath inside death visions of diaphanous carbon dioxide eyelid heaven? I don't think about this too long.

The dogs are fighting in the next room. I am considering rolling around in the backyard. Something must be done.

Something is making a noise—wait—now the noise has stopped. I have digressed, and will move on.

You're waiting for me to say something.

"Speech is a funny thing," I say out loud. My vocal cords rattle as I say this. "I am not saying this though." Wait. Maybe I did? "Things. Thins. Shins. Shingles. Single. Shimmering single shingles."

There's a wooden face on my wall with a plastic flower growing out of its head, glasses over its eyes, the flip-up kind, dark, a cigarette between its wooden lips, and a doo-rag on its head. But you already knew that.

Things are vibrating, but I'm tired of telling you things. I will tell you nothing.

The carpet feels like something.

I've officially lost the part of that thing which invents metaphors. Let's call him "Henry." "Henry" will tell you nothing.

Brass tails outside the halogen skin mind mime something about the nothing begging to know about the dancing blurs of the outside world. Outside, it's probably cooler, milder. Maybe there's a breeze— maybe there's something in the air screaming about the nothing, voiceless. Don't think about this too long.

I am disenfranchised outside of myself. Surely there must be things happening somewhere. Somewhere, someone must be dancing, and I would like to be watching, but I am not. Watching the dancing.

Although, in a way, I suppose I am. That is, I suppose I exist. I have been to college.

Ha. Rummy. Harmony. Hard running. Heart mumbling. Things about nothing. Voice lapses. Blue. Put on the blue dress, and pretend you exist; I will take you to dinner after we go dancing, but before we eat the couch. Ear the couch. Listen to the fibers without metaphor. Listen. List them. Lip's end. Lisps friend. Lifts tend. Liften. Lighten. Liken. Flowers?

Somewhere there are flowers. I will write about them later.

Somewhere there are flowers. It is slightly later. I won't go in to it any further anymore.

. . . .

In the morning I feel like absolute hell. I push my fingers into my skull, and try to plug up all the cracks. This does nothing, of course.

I wake up from dreams the moment something tethered is about to spring into action. This is a pattern with me; this is becoming a pattern.

All day toiling on inhumane typefaces. All night staring. All limbo dreaming.

All limbo dreaming. All limbo dreaming.

A ghost walks up to me after a film I haven't seen and asks: "didn't you leave these somewhere two, three years ago? Wouldn't you like to be somewhere, just this once?"

She tells me to wait for her in the funhouse. I do everything she says because I always listen to ghosts.

I'm waiting.

People who shouldn't remember me drop by and keep me company, and make the waiting trolley slow down irrevocably until I am in dawn's true limbo waiting with all the eternal waiting zombies, waiting and waiting.

Someone pulls out a Power Point presentation of my life. We all watch it together, waiting, and all the hair on my neck stands up, falls out, and drifts off in slow motion autumnal cubist textures.

The inside of my mouth forever tastes like fall. I've been rolling that taste over for ages. I can't get rid of it.

And so I'm tired now. And you won't let me go.

I am in dawn's true limbo, waiting, with all the eternal waiting zombies, waiting, waiting.

By the ankles. By the knees. By the waist. By the stomach. By the heart. By the eyes. By autumn. By Power Point. By dreaming. By dawn's true limbo—

By living, I'm learning how to disappear—I'm learning the texture of disappearing.

I hear footsteps. I tug on the lips of pure invisible violence until I catch teeth. I tear a chunk of skin from my left arm for something to blame the numbness on.

Funhouse mirrors and roller coasters are no good on gin.

I want to wake up, but I'm all out of orange juice. I want to wake up, and roll over ten years and see how this all turns out. It's the waiting that's killing me.

. . . .

I come home at night and there are people everywhere. Everywhere I've been all day, there have been people. I'm tired, and I don't want to talk about it.

I walk next door. The White Car invites me in, and reminds me of the bottle of vodka I left in her freezer a week ago.

"Jesus, I'd make the worst Marine."

She looks at me quizzically and shuffles through her crooked kitchen with the yellow tile and faint smell of burnt toast, fishing out a pair of shot glasses. I am staring through the plaid u-turns hidden beneath her pajama bottoms. I am driving somewhere, slowly, wishing I were being swallowed by fog and darkness. Thick, warm summer fog. Heavy August fog. Long, slender pale fogfingers.

I pour two shots. She yawns like a cat and stretches her right paw over her head.

"What are you doing tonight?" I ask her.

"You're looking at it."

"Do you want to go to the beach with me? I'm trying to get lost."

"Now? At night?"

"It's the best time."

"Can you drive?"

"Probably not." I pour another.

. . . .

The ceiling fan has stopped spinning. I would reach for it, but my arms aren't long enough. It hangs there in the air like something that would hang in the air—not the moon or the sun, because that is too obvious—unless they were x-shaped.

I try pleading with it for fifteen minutes. I watch the clock tick away time, and ask the ceiling fan why it doesn't favor movement anymore.

"You turned me off last night."

"You were rattling, asshole."

"Excuses, excuses. You'd make a terrible Marine."

Is it legal for someone on the June page of a calendar to be wearing white? It is before Labor Day. I color in Audrey Hepburn's shirt.

I wonder if I could strip all the color off the spines of the books behind my bed? They are mostly pale, faded versions of red or orange. Occasionally, there are some seriously disruptive teals, smoke-navy, goldenrod, aqua or library greens.

People on television have bowed heads and captions underneath their ties. I wonder—

They show a picture of Texas, and now it's raining.

It occurs to me that the world is spinning out of control, and that I am here asking my ceiling fan to keep up.

The faces on the television are smiling and happy now. They must have found the body.

I change the channel. Two men are sitting around a campfire. It occurs to me that I've never been camping.

Somewhere a door opens.

Henry walks in, still wearing his morning work clothes: a faded lime green t-shirt and a pair of khaki shorts. It occurs to me that I live in an urban vortex.

Henry opens the front door for his dog, who walks through the hall as if one of its legs is too long, then stumbles outside to crouch over the scorched, yellow

181

grass. He looks back at us, cross-eyed, with the horrified expression of a child caught masturbating.

I tell Henry about things. The toilet chain is broken. The orange juice in the fridge will help pacify his hangover. The world is spinning out of control, and my ceiling fan is not cooperating.

"Charlie, why didn't you take the blue pill like I told you to?"

"The bank teller said my account was overdrawn—and—it turns out my gun was a banana."

"I hate it when that shit happens."

. . . .

At night there are people everywhere. They rush in like water from a dam whose only weakness is moonlight.

I say "hello" and "no thank you," and go into my room to see what my ceiling fan has been up to.

It hangs there, silently. "You too?"

A thousand footsteps pound against the insides of my skull. Somewhere, someone is starting a fire. I wonder how long it would take them to make fog.

I open my window, fall out, and start my car.

. . . .

Most people wake up in the morning. I am one of them.

I get up and look outside. Still there.

I turn on the television to see if anything has caught on fire or fallen over. I lay there for a while thinking how different the world has become in the last few years. You didn't always have to wake up and make sure there is still a world, and that the sky isn't falling into a building somewhere.

These things are real now. These are real everyday things filmed in full Technicolor at unbelievable resolutions. I pour all my problems into an old sock, and throw them across the room.

. . . .

The White Car stops by. I am sitting alone in a room thinking about the possibility of breathing.

"I almost grabbed you last night," she says playfully. "I wanted to go to the beach. It's actually not a bad idea, and I wanted to get out. I kind of needed to—get out."

"I left around the time they started the forest fire."

"You seemed so upset, though. I was worried about you."

"*You* were worried?"

"Uh huh. I don't like seeing you like that."

"Wait, maybe I'm not emphasizing the right words—you were *worried*?"

"Is that really so hard to believe?"

"Well—yes. Yes, it is actually."

"Charlie, you should know me better than that."

"I'm—ah—sorry?"

"You should be."

"I might be."

"So, are you feeling better?" She is slow dancing with herself.

"Sure. Why not? What happened to you, anyway?"

"Well—I tried to grab you, but you—disappeared. So, I went next door to be by myself, and then everyone else followed me. And—I don't really know what happened after that. I was there with all these people and I just kind of lost it. I think I blacked out a little. I don't remember."

"Did you find the blue pill?"

"No. But someone gave me three yellows."

"That might have something to do with it. So what's up?"

"Oh, right! I'm having a misery party next door. I came by to see if you wanted to join me."

"Uh. Yeah. I'm in. Just let me get put on my team colors."

"Sweet. Hey, and I have wine."

"*You* have wine?"

"Yup."

"Then I'm definitely in."

I walk across the yard behind her, barefoot, trying not to watch her walk. I try to avoid sub-eye contact and inadvertent u-turns.

We watch movies on her couch, taking shots of vodka between glasses of cheap

white wine. Somewhere in between video love letters to Keira Knightly and Hugh Grant's inner monologue on men being islands, her new roommate with the megaphone voice and overlarge eyes comes home and says something I can't hear. The walls shake and my ears vibrate apart. The White Car and I nod, and I hand her the vodka.

Thirty seconds later Watson walks in, already drunk, and joins us on the couch.

The Megaphone's boyfriend also joins us. He feigns reluctance in shot glass wars, but eventually acquiesces after 3 ½ seconds of intense peer pressure, taking three in a row to catch up.

At midnight, we all go outside and play wiffle ball in total darkness. U-turns are unavoidable, but the fog is coming in nicely.

Eventually, The Megaphone and her boyfriend disappear inside, upstairs.

Watson defies six laws of physics, managing to sway while sitting down.

"Hey, Charlie, can I half ah nother shot?" he asks.

"Does everyday end in y?"

"I dunno. Maybe?"

"Here, man."

He spills half the glass on his shirt, and mumbles something to The White Car about stepping into the hallway for a second. She shrugs and follows him. I imagine he is either proposing marriage, or else threatening to join the circus if she doesn't dance with him immediately.

I sit on the couch in front of the arctic blast of the air conditioner, watching the clock and imagining things. How many elephants could they fit in a clown car? Do flaming hoops at the circus offend homosexuals? Do midgets have growth spurts? Five minutes pass. Six. Seven. Eight.

At twelve minutes, I imagine they've been carried off by radioactive pterodactyls. At fifteen, I think it must be pirates. At nineteen I'm sure of it. Fucking pirates.

At twenty minutes, the girl reappears, alone. Her eyes are slightly red, and I know everything Watson has said to her, even before she tells me.

"I just can't handle all this now. I…"

"I know. I know." I put my arms around her as she starts to sob. "This is some misery party, eh?"

She nods and hints at a thin smile.

185

"Look—he does this when he's drunk. You know that, right? He's drunk. He doesn't mean to say..."

"I know. It's just—it's just fucking everyone and everything right now. I just want to..."

"Disappear?"

"Yeah."

"I know the feeling."

"Can I have another shot?"

We have another shot. Then another. We are toasting to ceiling fans, the color blue, the smell of new paper and to life itself unraveling.

We are telling each other things. We are taking our skin off and getting drunk, talking like people talk when they're alone and made of liquid, and not facing a wall or dreaming about eyelashes.

We have another shot. She is telling me more things. True things. Whispered,

horrible, midnight full moon werewolf attack things—things rivaling the darkest, most

uncomfortable radioactive human fallout experiences ever dropped inside an

earlobe. I would burst, but luckily I am impervious to moonlight.

Every thirty seconds I get up to kneel by her chair and hold her still. I ease her head into the recess between my neck and shoulders, running my right hand across her back, wishing my fingertips had some sort of divine healing power, or at least a decent self-help section.

I wish I could push eject. I wish I could take all the things people carry with them away. I wish I could melt them off like ash from the end of a cigarette.

I pull her next to me on the couch, opening a blanket around her like a cape, and hold her as she finishes all her ghost stories. I don't know exactly where all of this is coming from, or even if we're still speaking English or have simply evolved in a telepathy of eyes, but I wholly understand the concept of unraveling. At least I can offer her that much.

I can't breathe but I don't want her to know. I've spent too much time doubting, wondering, falling, flickering, flaking, and imagining spilling her body onto the floor. Now, I'm actually looking through her eyes and discovering the loose wires of an actual human being. If I didn't know any better, I would propose, or threaten to run away with the circus as well.

Finally, when all the wind that carries her settles and she is herself, I realize how immaculately beautiful, tortured, tender and slight she is. I want to hold her so she doesn't blow away. I want all the impossible things possible. I want comic book powers or a better sense of humor.

I offer to trip over furniture. She laughs, and the planet slows and rolls into a ball.

Her legs fall over mine. She leans backwards, and falls into an invisible pool of couch death. I lay there, holding her. I lay there—stunned and awed. I have been moved. It has been a while. I assure myself I am breathing.

Her legs move while she sleeps. I think she's running.

I watch the clock. I close my eyes. I flutter and think better of fluttering.

I lift her legs over mine, and slip out. The air is thick and rich, like honey.

She stirs a little, but doesn't wake. I put my arms around her and kiss her neck. I try to say something. I don't.

I go home and slink into the corner of my bed. I can still feel her—her shape is stuck to mine.

"Goddamnit. Goddamnit. Goddamnit." Not her. She's not even real. She doesn't even have a name. She was born already on the blue pill. She must have stolen all these things from movies. Maybe her banana looked like a riffle.

She confided in me things no one should ever have to bare, and I suddenly envy Atlas, with his shoulders broad enough to hold up the entire world. Moreover, she almost convinced me that she's actually human.

"Goddamnit," I whisper to the walls. I would bang on them, but my entire body is numb.

Tomorrow morning I will have to wake up, and then what of her beauty? Not her. Not me.

My skin is vibrating, and her shape is stuck to mine. I pull a pile of pillows together into heaven, and curse all of man's innocence and naïve addition to beauty. I feel dumbly light, as if I were floating in space, and I am terrified of the repercussions of floating.

"Goddamnit."

The ceiling fan starts to spin.

. . . .

The next day I find her at home, laying on the couch, changing colors. A copy of my novel, closed, sits by her head.

188

I tell her I'm going away for the weekend. She nods and smiles, and I walk out backwards.

. . . .

It's raining again. I'm watching things grow heavier in the rain. Cars are slowing down. Trees are slumping. People are disappearing altogether.

Sometimes I can picture faces. If I close my eyes, I can almost see their outline. This one is smiling but not saying anything, as if I've already heard everything there is to hear, or as not to distinguish itself too much, or for all the other reasons people have expressions. I wonder about all the reasons. I count the rings around the tips of my fingers.

I stare into the dark recesses of all the imaginary eyes. It's raining, but I am growing lighter all the time. If I succeed to see whatever it is I'm imagining I'm looking at, I wonder if I will cease to exist altogether? Oh, but how I want to succeed.

Her hair is everywhere. I am running through fields of her hair. She is standing, just out of reach, sticking her tongue out at me.

I want to come closer. I want to bite it. I want to know if it tastes like copper.

"Copper?"

All the machinery of my brain stops.

"Never."

. . . .

I wake up on a foreign couch the day after a reading. I have to shake my head to remember.

189

There's a book on the table nearby. I open it, and it asks me things.

"Do you want to get breakfast?"

I look over to trace the voice and remember.

"No. No, I should really get going. Thanks..."

I put the book down, and gather my things in whatever arms I have left.

. . . .

I listen to things in the car on the way back home. Not just the naked rattle and hum and windshield whistle things, but music things. I have these obsessions with certain songs—they move in like western fronts, and weigh down my mind until I can reach in to pour all the water out.

I watch the road rolling under me as if I weren't moving at all. And, in fact, I'm not moving. I'm actually sitting on a thing spinning me across a world moving in a universe full of unknown amounts of rapid movement.

There's a Spiritualized song that is absolutely killing me. I play it over and over until I become a part of the song, or the song becomes a part of me, or of the unconscious flowing thing that Henry used to tell about in flat, careful voices.

All these songs—they part the clouds between my thoughts and shake all the rain off. They condense all the vast motion of the universe into little rhyming four-line stanzas.

I come down a little. I start to pour the water out.

But I can't help wanting to burst again—like I can almost peel all this skin off and finally be free. But free of what?

There is always space, and things seem to happen wherever there are spaces. This cannot be avoided. Only—maybe it's just all the pesky consciousness that bothers me.

Another shot of vodka? Are you trying to free me of my own mind? I would like that very much. Would you care to join me?

"Let's go to the beach."

"In the rain? But the sand will be so much heavier."

"It's the best time."

Right. Yes. Perhaps it is better to hide here for a little while longer, staring at the outlines of things I don't quite yet understand. Although—maybe I am starting to understand.

I'm almost home. Another turn. Steady. The road bends left, and I take it.

. . . .

Time passes. Sometimes time passes like wet streaks of light, sometimes it passes like gelatin wind. Sometimes, time passes like pieces of wooden soldiers caught in the fierce undertow of a flash flood.

. . . .

"What are you doing tonight?"

I look up.

"Hi." The White Car is standing in the doorway. Her eyes are concretely noncommittal. I could tell I her I am going to assassinate the president or play catch with the dog, and she'd just blink back and play

191

fetch either way. Should I tell her I'm starting a brothel in the basement? Should I hold auditions?

"You don't have a basement."

Right. "I don't know. Is the liquor store open on Sundays?" I ask.

We find a phone book under a pile of clothes in her living room. It's a little chewed up, but I find a number.

The liquor store *is* open on Sundays. In the next state.

The state line is twenty miles away. I drive, and The Megaphone tags along in the back seat.

I put the keys in the ignition and pause. "Look, whatever happens tonight, don't give me any more cigarettes, okay? My fucking throat is killing me. No more. Please. Okay?"

"Okay."

"OKAY."

"Thanks. So, does anyone know where this place is?"

"YEAH, YOU CAN'T MISS IT. IT'S ON THE LEFT."

"That narrows it down."

"YOU CAN'T MISS IT."

I stare at the girl on my right through the blurred corner of my eye. I want to tell her things.

I know she won't tell me things in front of other people. Not real things, anyway. She'll tell me where she went to eat or how much she drank last night, or who brought her a pack of baseball cards at two in the morning, but she won't tell me how her mother is, or if she knows why she runs in her sleep, or what she's running from.

No one says a word for twenty miles.

We pass by innumerable expanses of trees, some of them three times the size of houses, or bigger, all without saying a thing. We pass by the silent parade of dolphin nooses and solitary shoes, untied. We pass a car graveyard, a pet orphanage and a retirement home for used furniture.

My eyes marry the faded lines separating lanes in the highway. I feel sorry for them—I'd hate to be the thing keeping everyone else apart. I'd hate to be an ocean, a wall, a seatbelt or rational thought.

A strip mall hoists itself up over the horizon, and I know we must be getting close.

I park and leave the car running, sprint in, buy a large bottle of vodka, and hold the rewind button in all the way home.

The three of us start taking shots the second we're indoors. I take three in a row, straight up and sit back. Time slows down a little.

I want to say things—things about the other night. I want to ask her why she runs in her sleep. I want to ask her to dinner and to the moon. I look over at her with both eyes.

I have questions. I have empathy. I have hands. I have teeth. A tongue—

I take another shot.

We watch, together, as the television slows down.

Her phone rings. "Hello." Pause. "Yeah. Where are you?" Pause. "By the mall? The gas station?" Pause. "Okay. I'll be right there." Pause. "I'll be right back. Are you sticking around Charlie?"

"I'll be here."

I take another shot.

"I'll be right back…"

We sit for a while, The Megaphone and I, watching the television speak for us in slow motion bursts of colors and shapes. I have another shot.

"Can I have a cigarette?" I ask.

"YEAH, HERE."

After an hour of waiting, I walk back home across the yard.

Tim is sitting in the living room staring at bottom of an empty cardboard box.

"You're off?"

"Yeah. They let me go early," he says.

"Cool."

"Yeah."

"So—you wanna try something new"

"Yeah. Sure."

"These just came in..." I say, producing a shiny silver box filled with tiny packs of foil. Inside the foil packs are ten cards with 3D holographic images of the 1927 Yankees.

Henry is watching us. Henry doesn't do holograms anymore but he'll watch us play with them and advise us to look at things under varying conditions of light.

He tells us a story about things he's seen in holograms. Ten minutes pass.

"Anything?"

"A little." The world is just starting to vibrate. I open a third pack.

The White Car reappears with The Megaphone and Morticia Adams.

See? I don't need you to vibrate.

"What?"

"Nothing. Nothing at all."

"What are you guys doing?"

I hold out the shiny box.

"I don't know…"

"Oh come on. Don't make me peel away all the lines alone."

"What?"

"You'll be fine." Henry opens a pack for us, and studies it under the soft pulses of the kitchen light. He pulls out choice players, examining each one with determined scientific focus, and makes careful piles for everyone.

The girls each take a small stack.

"Can I get a cigarette from someone?"

We walk outside to smoke. I pass the remaining cards around.

Everyone chuckles a little.

"What are you shaking your head at?" I ask Henry.

"You're in for it now, Charlie."

"God, I hope so."

The five of us, minus Henry, walk across the yard.

I take a few steps in, and pause. The clock says it's 9:37. I can feel the air indoors beginning to conspire against me. I think it's starting to take on water.

I look at Tim as the girls disappear around the corner. "We'd better go outside, man. They'll figure it out soon enough."

"The bats?"

"The bats."

"Yeah. Woaw. Almost forgot about them. Good idea."

Tim and I stand in the backyard under an oddly-placed streetlight.

"Anything yet?"

"A little. Did the lights just flicker? Did they?"

The field behind us stretches out forever in the darkness.

I walk under the streetlight and look straight up. Little spots of white stardust flash and dissipate every few seconds. I think of trying to catch them; I hold my cup of water out towards the light.

I consider this.

I take a sip, turn my head, pause, and spit the contents out into a streaking mist. Tim starts laughing and can't stop. Then I start laughing. Then we're both rolling around in the grass, laughing hysterically.

We sit there for a while, on the ground, slowly becoming wary of gravity. Tim is chuckling again.

"What?"

He takes out his empty cardboard box, tosses it into the air, winks, and flashes me two cocked pistol hands, shooting them upward once and holding his pose. We're both laughing and rolling around in the grass.

Morticia Adams walks out into the backyard. Her eyes are visibly transparent, as if she's thinking about everything and nothing all at once. I wonder if *she'd* tell me things.

"Over here." I motion for her to join us.

"What?"

"Come over here. This streetlight is fantastic."

She walks over. Or glides. Or dances. Or floats. Her hips sway back and forth hypnotically, like the pendulum of an old clock.

She looks up. "Pretty." Her voice is raspy and small, like the echo of a voice.

"Can I have a cigarette?" I suddenly think my stomach might crawl out.

We sit down in the grass and play with the empty box, looking as determined as any four year old with an Astrophysics textbook possibly can.

"Look over there," I point to the bit of grass separating us from the field. It's filled with tiny white flowers, all about an inch high, and it makes the backyard look like a two-toned car, green and then white. "I just want to run my fingers across the tops. Like—maybe it would feel like water."

"Or fire..."

The lights flicker again.

"Did anyone see that?"

The other two walk out and sit with us. Everything has turned slightly orange.

"It's cold."

"Yeah."

Someone goes inside for sweatshirts and blankets. I close my eyes to watch the pendulum of time tick away, and I can feel my lips curling into a heavy, uneven grin.

Lips end. Lift then, and lighten. Flowers turn into water. Lights turn into faces.

I look back at everyone with both eyes. They are all conspicuously wrapped up like the tent scene at the end of E.T.

I say this out loud.

"Oh yeah."

"HAHA. WE DO!"

The girls are talking about something. Tim is playing with a fresh pack of baseball cards.

I stare at the wiffle ball bat by the doorway and wonder if I have any motor skills left. Everything is rushing by. I put the inside end of my elbow over my head, and push my eyes back in.

My stomach starts speaking in tongues. It's whispering something about revolt. It's forming a select committee and chartering a flight to the U.N. I take a deep breath and get up slowly.

"Have another." I breathe. Everyone breathes.

I find the wet white wiffle ball hidden in the grass just under Henry's bathroom window. The White Car hits first, swinging the bat and then herself into exaggerated circles before falling onto the ground, laughing.

Morticia Adams bats second, and sends the ball high over my head four times in a row.

"Did the lights just flicker?"

I bat third, and send the ball just into the chin-high grass of the field, and the game is over.

"Fucker!"

"YOU KILLED IT."

"I do things."

I am doing things. I go inside to borrow a Coke from the refrigerator, and it's like trying to walk through honey.

I walk back out backwards.

Everyone's sitting in a circle. A piece of something I don't remember eating comes free from the infinitely small space between my teeth. "Can I have a cigarette?"

Someone throws one.

"Fire?"

Tim hands me a lighter.

I can't turn the wheel over. My thumbs don't seem to be working. I spin it twelve times, cup my hand, then try again. Thirteen. Fourteen. Fifteen. I can feel the manic impetuousness of my body building shopping malls in between my fingers.

The girls are talking. Tim is rattling the cage a little.

I go inside to find the vodka. The clock says it's 9:48.

Tim is skulking around the backyard, gagging on something and stumbling around like some sort of agitated prehistoric beast that just discovered how to walk on two legs. The girls are hooded and laughing, huddled in the waiting room of an invisible post-millennial fall out shelter.

Time passes at a rate I can no longer control.

I'm staring at the field of wild summer wheat before us, grown nearly eye-level, towering well above us all, all sitting down.

"I wonder what's behind the grasses."

Things are flickering.

"I don't know. Midgets?"

"Midgets would be great right about now. With weapons."

"Midgets with axes hiding in the grasses."

"No!," Tim shouts, annoyed.

"How does a midget hold axes? No, wait. How *do* Midgets hold axes? Does? Do?"

"They keep them in their asses. There are midgets in the grasses with axes in their asses. Just over the passes."

Everyone falls over, laughing. I spit Coke-rain into the air.

"Look—that cat is sniffing gases."

There's a cat under one of the cars in the driveway, tailing at the tail pipe. We watch it for hours. I try to catch it, but can't remember how to use my legs. I hold out my Coke.

Hours.

The Megaphone's boyfriend pulls up, and the cat runs off. I catch him up on vodka. He and the girl curl into a blue blanket in front of us.

I whisper to the others, "don't nobody tell him about the midgets with the axes in their...."

"What?"

"They're hiding in the grasses."

"What are you gu..."

"Don't mind us. We've been sniffing gases."

Morticia Adams and The White Car take shots with me.

"Hey Charlie?" the White Car asks.

"Yesss..."

"You wanna fo gor a walk?"

I look over at the skulking tar pit victim and pair of flickering orange figures on the blue blanket to my right, and decide I'd better.

I help the two girls up and ask for a cigarette. My throat crawls out, and goes home for the night.

I close my eyes, and watch the pulsing, red pendulum of time. It takes us about an hour and a half to navigate our way to the front yard. There's a tree in the way, and it's got arms. There are rocks in the driveway, and they won't stop breathing.

Morticia walks out into the street, cups her hands together, and dances down the median strip like a blind gypsy. The White Car and I almost make it to the edge of my house, about fifty yards or so, before we both start wandering off in other directions. I wonder if this is how Columbus felt.

"We'll never find the spices this way."

"What?"

"Orange! Did you see that? The flickering..."

A car is coming toward us.

Morticia makes a graceful spin into a stoic L-shape. "I'm a tree."

The White Car folds herself in half and disappears into the front lawn. "I'm a rock."

I stand still and wave like an Animatronic hamburger mascot.

We do this several times as traffic intermittently interrupts our belly dancing spice rout. Trees, rocks, mailboxes, fence posts, lawn gnomes, boxwoods, blankets, birch arms, burger mascots and belly dancers.

We sit in the driveway between both houses, staring at a strange hollow light filtering through the fence across the street, and spilling out into odd shapes in the road.

Morticia looks up excitedly. "Oh! Do you have any more of that canvas?"

I do.

"Charcoal?"

"Yesss…"

"Can you?"

"I can always try."

I ring the bell, and take the L train to the front door. Tim is passed out on the living room couch, his head facing the wall, and the rest of him rolled into a tiny ball like a cat. I rummage through a tangled closet and pull out four thin sheets of foam-core and a small rectangular package of charcoal crayons.

The girls sit in the front yard, legs folded Indian-style, frantically sketching out the amorphous light shapes like a pair of resolute preschoolers. I lay on my back, soaking up all the evening dew in the grasses.

I shake my head and laugh. "We'll never find India at this rate."

"I don't care!"

Hours.

Inside, we drain the rest of the vodka and attempt to make cheeseburgers on an old stove that could've passed for an extra in a low budget 1980's horror movie.

It's finally later now. The alcohol has fixed time.

Morticia has procured a shovel and is digging through the couch for her keys. We watch her, The White Car and I, the last two human beings alive, and consider the idea of forming a committee to possibly discuss the eventual consideration of calling for a vote on helping.

"Did you look outside?"

We all look outside.

There's a graveyard of blankets, hooded sweatshirts, and empty cigarette packs under the hushed hum of my once flickering streetlight, but there are no keys. We follow the girl and her invisible shovel arm around outside and back through the house, offering the occasional suggestion.

"Did you look in your pockets?"

"Yes. Yes. Yes. Six times. I need to find them. If I'm not home…"

"She'll turn into a pumpkin?"

"Look—it's already started…"

"Do you think she'd let me touch her stem?"

"Charlie!"

She circles the house six more times, stapling furniture on the ceiling for good luck, and rearranging the couch into a spice rack.

"Finally!"

"What?"

"Jenga!"

"Bastards!"

The White Car and I fall against the same wall and clutch our sides, but not each other's.

"Hey, look, do want a ride? I think I've got most of my motor skills back."

"But my keys…"

"Well—can you break in?"

"Maybe. Yes. Maybe. Let's. Do you mind? Thank you. Yes!"

I convince myself I can navigate the streets. It's usually a straight shot when you're straight, but everything's always little different when the world is orange, flickering, vibrating, and slowly turning into honey. I take turns on training wheel wings, running stop lights and stoping at ceiling fans. We pass a cop car by the shadows of a school parking lot and hold our breath.

"Here. Turn left."

I turn left, and pull up unto the curb at the side of a small one-story house. Morticia Adams runs out— through the yard over a dull chain link fence—and belly dances her way onto the back porch, disappearing completely, forever.

I think of waving. I think of a lot of things. I drift backwards, careful to avoid ceiling fans.

I sneak down the highway. I may, indeed, be invisible. I am large, and contain multitudes of liver damage.

It's quiet inside The White Car's house. I tiptoe through the hall and find her passed out on the couch, alone, covered by a dull white web of blankets in the darkness. I want to say things, but there isn't anyone left to say them to.

I take the last shot in the bottle and walk across the yard, home.

It's almost dawn. I stare at the oddly-placed flickering ghost streetlight one last time. It doesn't vibrate anymore, so much as it quietly watches me and eulogizes. I suddenly feel like the last survivor of that aforementioned low budget 1980's horror movie.

I lock the door behind me, and am immediately consumed by a tornado of dense blue blankets.

. . . .

In the morning, which is to say, the late afternoon, every driveway in the world is vacant.

I find a pile of foam-core canvases stacked up on the side of the house. Each one seems to have the same series of long, indecipherable black lines scrawled across the surface.

This is all that is left.

. . . .

I wonder about other people's identities. Is everyone like this? Is there a Clark Kent and a Superman inside everyone—a truth found only in the skies, or in phone booths? A cape persona, and a baseball card persona?

She is getting to me. There's a white car double parked in the opening credits of my thoughts.

When she is human, when she tells me things about herself, the things that make her shiver, she fills up endless canisters of film with her shivering. Other times, she seems as cinematic as a mannequin fixed to a wooden frame.

More than anything, the fact that she is getting to me is getting to me. If she looked a twist less like perfection, would I bat an eyelash? Would I give her humanity the benefit of the doubt? Would I stay awake all night just to watch her shiver? Are both sides part of the same person, someone trapped in the confused duality of being young, or am I just another thing to be played off—as if, this one likes the whore, this one the saint, this one the secret work of art that only I truly know about?

Is everyone like this? Is Eve like this? Is Tim? Am I? Are we even old enough to know if the opening credits of our own individual humanity has a side, or casts a shadow, or creates a rift?

I always thought that I was the same person from the first to the last page—that my growth was only the mere focusing of the lens of the microscope I put on things—that I never change—that only the way and the clarity which I see the world gets better by the end.

But maybe I've been sleeping all along. Maybe I've been lying to myself that I'm—that anyone—is really in the process of waking up.

. . . .

VIII. No Surprises.

On Tuesday I ship five books to a small independent book store in Washington D.C., and one to my uncle in Denver. On Wednesday I sell a quarter of a box of baseball cards to my own mother, and on Thursday, I write three poems no one will ever read unless I simultaneously die, become famous, and am burglarized.

Being an artist rarely makes any sense to anyone other than the artists themselves. And why should it? What possible rational motivation could there be to pursue the most tried and failed profession in modern history—one that can't be helped by any amount of college degrees, or be learned or taught through any sort of coherent system? Luck is our only master. To succeed, or even survive, you must be lucky enough to single-handedly declassify some previously unknown corner of the human soul while still retaining enough magic to alter the very fabric of time and space itself to bring enough of the wallet-carrying populous together to champion you.

You cannot expect or anticipate this; you cannot expect to live through any manipulation of art. You can only obey the voices, the thing that talks you out of sleep, out of hunger, out of being rational altogether.

If I knew how to do anything else, I would never write another word, and I don't fool myself into thinking I am a serviceable salesman because I move baseball cards to people in the next room. Baseball cards move themselves—I am merely a conduit. I am merely lucky enough to be in the next room when someone needs a good fog.

You try to do the same as an artist; you try to be lucky, you try to be patient, and you must be humble and willing to starve for extended periods with little or no warning. You must be willing to disappear completely—you must accept that this is the most likely thing that will ever happen once you start giving in to the voices.

You must be ready to accept the fact that you are mad to attempt any of this; you are mad, and more than likely, society will never forgive you for it.

. . . .

I am sitting in a room with a girl who has no name. She is telling me things.

I kiss her. I fall sideways into honey, and kiss the words out of her perfect little flapping mouth. I lick all the salt off of her perfect little flapping tongue. I close my eyes and vanish for a second.

"Charlie…"

I am awake.

"Charlie—we shouldn't. Why did…"

"I couldn't think of a reason not to anymore."

"Charlie, I—don't—think—I don't think of you like *that*."

This is me breathing.

"Charlie?"

"Yeah? Sure. No, It's fine. It's all fine."

"I'm sorry."

"It's okay. That's all I really needed."

"Charlie, are you hungry?"

"Always."

. . . .

208

I am driving. I can tell, because there's a car underneath me.

The box of books in my passenger seat ask me if we can't stop to use the bathroom.

"I'll look for something," I tell it.

"That's all I really needed," it says, a little mockingly.

We laugh, the box of books and I.

We pass by things together. We pass by sunsets and dooryards. We swerve to avoid a raindrop. We stop at a McDonald's to use the bathroom. We pass by all the people not stopping to use the bathroom, and wonder why they're allowed to have eyes.

We make up stories about the people we pass on the road.

We move across the earth that is already moving so fast that we don't notice anything moving at all.

· · · · · · · · · ·

Tim and I walk through a park just outside of town, passing a pack of baseball cards back and forth. I tell him about things.

"She said that?"

"She did."

"And you said *that*?"

"I think I might have."

"That's funny."

"It was true."

"I'm sorry, but what did you expect? I mean, from her?"

"Tim, I never expect anything. It's the only way you can get by without being a constant disappointment to yourself."

"God, I wish I could laugh at that."

"Me too."

"So did you sell any books yesterday?"

"Not a fucking thing."

"Did you sell any of the *other* thing?"

"Almost half a box."

"Well, I guess it wasn't a total loss."

"Hardly anything is ever a *total* loss. And if it is, they still serve alcohol in public places."

"Good point."

. . . .

Tim and I are sitting in a public place.

Graham walks in and orders the cheapest beer on tap. I raise my five dollar rum and coke, and we clank glasses.

The band is playing a song that's so familiar, it's unrecognizable. Tim squints at them and shakes his head.

Two college girls wearing giant free parking signs float in and land a few seats away from us. We watch gravity reorganize itself around them.

A tall, skinny kid with a crew cut puts his arm on the rail in front of them, and cracks what's easily the third phoniest smile I've ever seen. The girls nod gravely as the mirror behind the bar fractures his reflection into a trillion pieces.

A pair of wild hand gestures helicopter by, barely stopping. The girls blink and yawn like a pair of mute puppies.

We are watching them without watching them.

The band takes a break. This is me breathing.

"I needed that."

"What's that?"

"Silence. This is the best song they've played all night."

"Aww man!" Graham groans, and starts laughing. He pauses to look up at the ceiling, and gets lost in something that makes him start laughing again, harder and harder, until his face hiccups and disappears.

"Is he all right?"

"He's great. I sold him a half box yesterday."

Tim laughs a broken tenor. We all clank glasses.

A bouncer walks in and ropes off the dinosaur graveyard in front of the two girls, who I'm still not convinced breathe oxygen. I look down at my empty glass.

"You guys want to split?"

"Yeah, sure."

"Yeah, in a minute…"

Graham and Tim simultaneously raise their glasses and stare sheepishly at the two pretty gargoyles.

"Go talk to them. There's two of you, two of them…"

"Fuck, I haven't got anything to offer *them*."

Tim agrees.

"Fuck, they're just college girls."

"Yeah, but there's steam coming out of their waistlines."

"So, offer them free baseball cards and invite them back to your place. We're going there anyway."

"Are we?"

"It's closer than Vegas."

"By miles."

"Still. I wouldn't know what to say to *that*."

"D'you want me to talk to them? Fuck, everyone else here's tried."

"And failed miserably. Look, I've been keeping score." Graham points to several dozen fresh hashmarks on the bar.

"There's nothing to lose then, is there?"

I move three barstools to the left. The brunette looks at me first.

"Yes?"

"Hey, are you two sticking around?"

"Uh—yeah."

"Cool."

I walk away as they tilt their heads sideways like Labradors.

"Let's go guys."

. . . .

IX. Such Great Heights.

Eve is having a party.

Graham hands me a cigarette as we walk through the front door, swing through the kitchen, and hang a left into the garage.

There's a bucket of sand and a graveyard of ash by the door. We count the rings in the air to catch up on what we've missed.

Henry's girlfriend Rosalyn has just moved in with Eve, and is starting to invade her wall space with paintings. I wander through a room of frowning portraits where Henry is a gaunt authoritarian, three European countries meaner and forty pounds lighter than he ever was, and Eve is stuffed into a bleak fireplace with a mouthful of duct-tape and Jenny Saville thighs.

I pour a glass of whiskey—because my contract considers this a public appearance.

A girl with frenetic silver eyes and short, choppy hair dyed bright purple sits in the living room examining a copy of my book. Her expression resembles something caught in a thunderstorm.

I hand her an umbrella and sit down across the room, just close enough that she notices how hard I'm working to look inconspicuous.

"I hear it's terrible," I tell her. "There isn't much of a plot, and the protagonist never really develops a consistent or believable voice."

"Funny. So, what's it like writing an entire book?" she deadpans.

"How did you…"

"There's a picture of you on the back cover."

"Right. Well, fuck. What did you think? Did you read any of it?"

"A little. It's interesting. How many chapter subheadings have you stolen from Radiohead lyrics?"

"Oh good, you hate it."

"It's all right. Answer the question."

"Uh—I don't—really—know. Let me see." I flip through a few chapters. "Looks like it's just the one. Nice catch though."

"I'm Gretchen."

"Charlie."

"Yeah, I know."

"Right. I think I need a drink..."

Graham is waiting for me in the kitchen. I fish a pair of fresh mugs out of the kitchen cupboard, and pour two glasses of straight vodka.

"Here you go. One vodka martini."

Graham nods and laughs a little. His face hiccups, but doesn't quite disappear.

"Here's to the systematic disordering of the senses."

"Cheers," Graham laughs.

Piera floats in through the back door and hovers for what might be days. All the light in the room is sucked into the black recesses of her cartoon eyes. Graham hangs on a nearby light fixture, shivering.

"Hey, did you ever hook up with that VCR?"

"Fffssssshhhhhhhhhhhttttttt."

Gretchen is sitting on a small yellow couch that faces the front wall of the living room, whispering something to a girl who looks far too much like a swollen Piera Bella.

I have a seat next to Gretchen, and am introduced to Swollen Piera and her roommate, who I'm led to believe is both homosexual and Mormon.

"He has special underwear," Gretchen fills me in.

"Oh yeah? Does it give you powers?"

"No. Oreos give me powers."

"Like Popeye?"

"Yeah. Only, I haven't quite figured out how to squeeze the bag over my head without getting a lapful of crumbs and a nice cookie crown."

"So what's the Mormon underwear for?"

"It's sort of like our cross. No—just kidding. I dunno…"

"Don't superheroes usually wear their underwear outside their clothes?"

"Not Mormon superheroes. I mean, you have to draw the line somewhere."

"Right…"

"He fights ninjas." Gretchen and Swollen Piera cup their hands over their chuckling mouths in hysterical alcoholic laughter.

Henry shows up late, dressed in the same green shirt and blue jeans he's wearing in the Hitler painting. I raise my glass. He sways a little and falls, face first, onto the carpet. I tuck a few jokes away for later, and head into the kitchen for a spatula.

Graham climbs down off the light fixture to examine the stereo in the living room.

"You Deejaying tonight?"

"Might as well. Man, I'd like to talk to that girl Piera, but I don't speak *statue*."

A little voice drifts across the room, "d'you have any Mormon superhero music?"

"Uh—I can check."

"What's wrong with Piera?"

"Nothing. Nothing that I can tell." Graham hiccups, and tucks his face into his hands.

"I hear they have baseball cards in the basement. Go check it out. Get your head straight."

"Or crooked," he laughs. "Good idea."

"Hey, whatever works. Here—take the spatula, and bring Henry with you."

Gretchen and Swollen Piera are on their way out the door. I catch them in the driveway, and hand each of them a paperback.

"I'm told it makes an excellent coaster."

"See you around, Charlie," Gretchen says thoughtfully.

Graham and Henry leave right behind them, one carrying the other.

Abrams walks in five minutes later. She sees me, and heads straight for the basement without blinking.

Downstairs, in the far corner of Eve's cavernous underground, the few remaining survivors sit around playing Trivial Pursuit with a fresh twelve pack and enough random bottles of liquor to cripple an English rugby team.

We throw away the board and pass the questions around, yelling out answers and shoving shots of liquor into the laps of the defeated.

Abrams sits across from me, shoving drinks my way and hinting at the thin gleam twinkling in her right eye.

Watson's cousin is there, slumping against a wall with a girl who keeps reminding us that she absolutely *has* to get up early tomorrow, "to save lives."

"What are you, a doctor?"

"Nurse."

"Want a shot?"

"Absolutely!"

Eve and Rosalyn yawn by the stairwell. Three extras with randomized party avatars sit in the opposite corner, eying whatever's left alive. I don't even know their names enough to compete with them, but the world is underwater and I have my own private reservation gleam.

Other people have started to notice that the world is underwater. English, once the official language, has succumbed to a parade of crooked eyebrows and imaginary life preservers.

The three party avatars elbow each other and squint into the basement twilight. I stick a flag in Abrams's inner thigh and wave to the camera.

Eve and Rosalyn go to bed, and Watson's cousin and the nurse excuse themselves in favor of late night fast food death.

Abrams and I are still locked in a staring contest on opposite day.

There are things I've wanted to say to her—there are utter, simplistic, ordinary, easy, nominal things, and there is that elusive sentence, "I had a really good time the other night," that I've dodged for weeks. But maybe I can avoid words altogether tonight.

"What is the capital of Paraguay?"

"Uruguay?"

"Paraguay city?"

"New question."

She pours another beer down her throat and looks at me for a fleeting moment that seems to sum up our entire nonexistent relationship.

One of the stragglers stumbles upstairs and outside through the back door and we can faintly make out the sound of his stomach calling for a mulligan.

The other two check on the consistency of the front porch while Abrams and I trail behind them.

I catch her in the driveway. "Where're you going now? It's still kind of early."

"I'm going to my car. It's just across the street."

"Let me give you a lift."

"Nah, I'll walk. It's not that…"

"Come on, it's no trouble. In fact, I insist."

"No thanks Charlie. Goodnight."

I wait for her to turn around, but it never happens.

The world is Atlantean.

I swim to my car, turn the engine over, and listen to ungraceful sound of the explosion going off under the hood. I punch the wheel. My hand throbs a little. I punch it again, harder.

The clock tells me its 3:43 a.m.

. . . .

There's a note on the door telling me to *"call Kyle."*

"Who the fuck is Kyle? Hey Watson…"

Watson is sitting on the couch watching a man wrestle an alligator.

"Who the fuck is Kyle? What's this note about?"

"Some kid keeps calling."

"What kid?"

"Some college kid. Wants *the usual*."

"You know I'm dry."

"I know. I just told him you'd try. It could open up the college market..."

"What does he want, just a few packs?"

"I don't know. I think so."

"Look, I'll do what I can. If I can get anything I'll leave it on my desk. Give him *the usual* first timer rates. I'm going out."

. . . .

The next morning, I call Eve and try to wrestle Gretchen's phone number away from her. She plays dumb, but tells me she might make an appearance at another soirée at her place. I tell her I'll be there with batwings on.

Rosalyn calls not long after to poke around. I can tell she is prying, because she sounds like a small child on a swing set; her voice is rising and kicking in the wind, dancing and jumping out of her throat. She tells me Gretchen is a painter, newly single, and that I've been mentioned as a possible human being who breathes the same type of oxygen and is made up of various similar subatomic particles.

"Should I wear my suit of armor?"

"No, nothing like that. But maybe iron a shirt, Charlie."

"Do what to a what?"

I talk to Watson about the possibility. He encourages me and I think of not inviting him to the party.

Graham and I walk in a few hours later, and I immediately pour myself a mug of vodka.

Gretchen is sitting on the couch, making the air a little heavy. A copy of my book glares at me from the coffee table.

"Copper?"

"Shhh..."

I make a vague attempt to sit down in the most casually ambiguous, evasively noncommittal way possible.

"Hi." My voice cracks. Three or four painfully ordinary words escape my lips and run for the door, sorely aware of the low pressure system surrounding us which may, at any given moment, turn into rain.

"You know, you weren't this hard to talk to when you were a stranger clutching my picture, and I was drunk," I say.

"That was good Charlie, now try it out loud."

"What? Oh fuck, you're not telepathic are you?"

"Not yet."

"I saw your paintings," I finally manage. "Ros showed me the website."

"Yeah? Don't judge me on that—it was pretty thrown together."

"No—I liked the work a lot; I liked the progression. I like how everything was dated, and you could see—well—you could see the progression from the sort of impressionist work you started on years ago, to the more—sort of—experimental stuff you're doing now. I really liked the latest two. I'm pretty impressed, actually."

"Much better. Now try being human."

"Fuck..."

She tells me about the long, peculiar process in which she works. There are questionnaires and slide shows, photographs and digital manipulation, a slow waltz and a frantic Argentinian tango. Finally, she converts everything back to analogue by making an oil painting. I don't hide the fact that I'm a little impressed.

She hands me a rum runner to wash out the vodka.

Watson shows up with several 40's already tucked into his liver. He grabs a bottle of rum and immediately attempts to chat up Gretchen.

"No, really. I mean, I *love* Lionel Ritchie. I'll admit it. I *love* how *positive* his music is. I think everyone should try to have a *positive* impact on the lives of those around them."

I choke on my drink a little and laugh—I already know where he's going with this.

"What?"

"Watson, man, I think everyone wants to have a positive influence on the world. Unless you're a fucking terrorist—or maybe a lawyer. I think it's like announcing you're carbon based."

"No, seriously."

"Right."

"What?"

I stare at him for a minute—his eyes are prematurely crossing. He shrugs at me.

"What?"

"Nothing."

He and Gretchen go off into the basement together.

If I shook my head anymore it would have to be legally reclassified as a propeller.

"Look on the bright side; you'll save a ton on gas."

"Fuck…"

Graham and several others hobble downstairs.

It occurs to me that everything has become a competition. Only, I don't feel like playing wiffle ball again. Not anymore. Not tonight.

I walk back into the living room where Rosalyn and Eve are digging through a large, black portfolio of artwork they've done over the last year.

Eve looks a little concerned.

"Hey? Charlie, what's the matter?"

"Nothing."

"Watson?"

"He wants to have a *positive* effect on *eeeehhhveryone*," I say. "Fuck…"

"Where's Gretchen? I thought the two of you were hitting it off."

"Yeah, me too. She's downstairs. Watson went off on one of his drunken rants about how he's going to be the next fucking Dali Lama, and I think she bought it. I just don't feel like trying to talk over him tonight."

Rosalyn looks up and whispers, "damnit, I told him to lay off of her. He's completely wrong for her."

"Yeah. I kind of told him I was into her too, but I don't think he's really firing on all cylinders at right now. Oh, unless you've got ethanol…"

"Guys are weird. If a girl did that to me, I'd probably claw her eyes out."

"Well, actually, I'm completely thrilled," I say.

"Seriously though—he knew about this. And he's supposed to be your friend! I'd be out for blood."

"Thanks, but I've eaten."

"Well, don't take it so hard. You're a great person Charlie. He doesn't deserve friends like you."

"Hey, remember that time I saved Christmas?"

222

"Why don't you just grab her, and ask her to go for a walk?"

"I don't know. Isn't that a little presumptuous?"

"Screw presumptuous!" Eve pauses and gets serious. "You've got to go on the attack, Charlie. I mean, that's how it works."

"Fuck it. I just don't feel like it. I don't really feel like forcing myself on anyone or—I don't know. I kind of figured I'd just try playing myself for the evening."

"But he's so wrong for her…"

The girls start cataloging a list of Watson's faults on a nearby chalkboard, and as much as I'd love to stay and clap, I don't really feel like condemning old friends right now. In fact, I don't really know what I feel like anymore.

I wander outside and light a cigarette.

The night has washed away most of the heaviness in the air. There are even a few stars out. I stand under a wilting pine tree, looking up, trying to grasp the distance until I nearly lose an arm to a swarm of mosquitoes.

The living room is empty. I sit on the floor and raid the CD player.

Swollen Piera makes a dull, cold shadow over my back. I shiver a little.

"Hey, that's a great shirt."

"Thanks."

"What do you call that color?"

"Uh, it's called black."

"Interesting. So, what are you doing?"

"Saving Christmas."

"Are you okay, Charlie, is it?"

"Yes. I am a *great* person," I say mechanically.

"Well, good for you. Are you coming downstairs?"

"I don't think so."

"Hey, is there something you want to talk about?"

"No thanks."

"You look a little troubled."

"Yeah, well, I'm playing myself for the evening."

"Well, good for you."

I refill my mug of vodka.

Gretchen comes in and sits down next to me. She's saying something, but I'm not listening anymore. I study her face, and think about allowing myself to wonder what her lower lip tastes like. I wonder if she's ever drank vodka from a coffee mug? I wonder if she'd ever let me stare off into her frenetic silver eyes without getting the urge to run for the door? Would anyone?

A half hour later, she goes into the kitchen to refill her drink, I hear Watson again, his voice swelling even louder, talking about how incredibly dark he is and advising Eve that she should learn to paint like Gretchen, whom he calls a "genius."

I shake my head, and am fined by the FAA.

Eve and Ros walk in and assure me they are furious. They list off, not only Watson's growing list of faults, but all my wily charms like basic human kindness and my deft ability to breathe oxygen. And I love them for it—I really do—but I'm not here to listen to my qualifications for pope. I just wanted the girl. I just wanted a nice, artistic, bright, lovely, challenging girl, and I just wanted to be honest about it for a change. I am making the least out of my silly, uneven, erratic beast.

Graham walks in and puts his hand on my shoulder, wordlessly.

We drive back to the house. I complain openly— probably even a little brazenly— and at the same time I want to strike myself for doing so.

Graham, as always, has been through all of this, and tells me stories to back it all up. He understands, but reminds me again and again that all's fair. I put the gun down, and stare off at the eggshell treetops that streak by.

At the house, White Car pulls up just as Graham speeds off.

"Hey! Do you have any extra baseball cards on you?"

"Hey Charlie. Fuck yeah I do! Why, d'you want to come inside and open a pack?"

"Yeah. Let's go inside. I need a little sympathy from the devil."

. . . .

When I finally crawl back home, a little email alert blinks at me from the corner of my computer. It is an apologetic letter from Gretchen. It is a short one.

I reply—briefly—that the world is fine and ask her to do something as insignificant as coffee, or having mass and taking up space.

In the morning, there is a reply that simply says, "yes."

. . . .

Watson stands in the doorway, slouched, a thin, wry grin stirring at the corners of his mouth.

"What's up, buddy?" he asks.

"Nothing. Nothing at all."

"Are you—like—pissed off, or something?"

"No. Why would I be pissed off? What the fuck could you have done to piss me off?"

"What, that girl?"

I look up at him. I freeze.

"Man, I was I just talking!"

"You talk too much."

"Man, you're really…"

"But you never really say anything, do you?"

"What're you…"

"Oh, fuck off, will you? Just fuck right the hell off. She might have been *just a girl,* but I *liked* this one. I actually fucking liked this one. And I told you that. And you follow that admission by spending an entire night playing monopoly on her eardrums with your fucking inane thoughts. *I'm so dark. I want to have a positive effect on everyone. I like Lionel Ritchie.* Christ, you might as well have told her you like long walks on the beach and your father is fucking Santa Claus."

"Man, I don't even remember any of that shit."

"That's the fucking point—theres nothing to remember. It was just your usual inane nonsense."

Watson nails his arm to the doorway with his fist. "Hey, fuck you Charlie. I had every right…"

"Yes. You had every right to be a jackass. You had every right to disrespect an old friend. You had every right to say you liked Lionel Ritchie."

"I do like Lionel Ritchie."

I slam my right hand against the wall. All the dust falls off the ceiling and chokes the air. "Oh, fuck off. Fuck right off. Get the hell out of my goddamned room before I smash something over your fucking head."

I stare through the emptiness of his eye sockets and shoot laser beams through his skull. He stares back defiantly, but no one moves; no one moves, but the incandescent dust in the air.

"Fuck Lionel Ritchie."

"Whatever," Watson peels his arm off the doorway, "you've lost a fucking friend, Charlie."

. . . .

Tim and I are driving.

I sit in the passenger seat as Tim and I circle the town, talking about all the indecisions and revisions which a moment will reverse.

"You said that to him?"

"I did. I said, *fuck Lionel Ritchie*. And, boy did I mean it."

"That's funny. How did you say it? Were there veins in his forehead?"

"There were, but I shot them out with lasers."

"That's funny. He probably fucking deserved it."

"Probably."

"So—what d'you think's gonna happen?"

"I don't know…"

Someone is standing on the back porch when we pull up—someone I don't recognize.

There's an older man pacing the yard as well, maybe mid-forties. His skin looks like a cheap leather handbag, and his eyes look like the eyes painted on cartoon missiles. I get the distinct impression they're not here to challenge us to a game of badminton.

I tell Tim under my breath to be on guard. He nods and cracks a knuckle.

"Hey. What's up?"

"Hey, Charlie is it? I'm Kyle. And this is my old man…"

I stick out my right hand and manage the first syllable of "hello" just as Leatherface harpoons me with his mammoth fingers and pulls me up off the ground, throat first.

I gag and feel my eyes pop out. Leatherface squints, and lifts me higher while his free hand punches a bright red hole into the side of my head.

"Now, what do you have to say for yourself you little fuck?"

"Haghk? Freedom?"

"Listen, you little asshole—you sold my son and me a bum pack. There wasn't even a single starting pitcher! We want our fucking money back, and we want it right now. Got it?"

I gasp, and manage to get just enough spit through my lips to wet his hands. He hammers my head again.

I start to lose light.

I think I hear someone yelling something. I fall to the ground and cough sand.

"NOW GODDAMNIT!"

Tim stands behind the two of them on the porch completely stunned and frozen. I stumble to my feet and limp inside, through the front door and into my room, and fish out a fresh pack.

"Here," I throw it at him, "here's another pack. I didn't know the deck was even fucking short. I gave it to you just as I got it. Fuck! I wasn't even here! But fuck it. Fuck you! Whatever. We're even. Now get the fuck out of here, get the hell off my lawn and leave me the fuck alone." My voice cracks. I rub the large red dent in my throat.

"Hey, look, we're sorry for coming on like this man, but we just don't like getting ripped off, you see? I've got to look out for my boy."

"Yeah, I'm sure that *Father of the Year* plaque is in the mail. Whatever. Thanks. Bye."

"Hey, listen. Wait. Hey, man, do you happen to have another box?"

"Fuck! Fuck you. Jesus Christ. Yeah. Sure it's a hundred fucking dollars." I throw a worn cardboard rectangle at him. "Here. Now I don't ever want to fucking see you here again."

"Hey listen, do you mind if we hit the ATM and run right back? Won't be ten minutes…"

"Fuck. Sure. Whatever. Goddamnit," my voice breaks, "this is the last fucking time, *got it?*"

"Yeah, yeah. That's cool, man. Look, hey we're real sorry we had to come like that, but I didn't know how resistant you'd be."

"Yeah, well it's a little hard to be resistant when you're six feet off the ground and can't breathe."

"That's the first thing they teach you in the Marines."

"Good to know. Goddamnit, go! Ten minutes. I'm fucking counting…"

. . . .

Tim and I stand in the kitchen.

"I'm so sorry Charlie—I didn't know what to do. If that guy had a knife or something and I'd charged him, he could have gutted you. Probably me too. That guy was fucking crazy."

229

"I think he broke my vocal cords," I manage. I start laughing. I don't even know why, but now I can't stop.

. . . .

Henry wakes me up when he gets home. "We have to talk."

"Gee, whatever about?"

"Your career options."

"Oh?"

"Look—I was talking to somebody today—and they laid out what can happen to you when they find baseball cards in your house."

"..."

"The point is, I don't want you selling anymore. I've got to be more careful. I..."

"Don't worry about it. I quit."

"You what? Hey, what the fuck happened to your eye?"

"Freedom punched me in the fucking face. Thanks for noticing."

"You're not making any sense..."

"Look, what's this really about Henry? My moral renaissance, or Watson's fucking pride?"

"Look, you know I don't appreciate what you did to Watson, but..."

"What I did to him? Huh. You come in here with some fucking sermon, but really you're kicking me out because Watson got hammered and we had it out about a girl? You fucking hypocrite, you were my best fucking customer."

"Well, things change."

"They sure do. You know, your timing is just fucking impeccable."

"Look, this has got to happen."

"I told you, I already quit."

"Charlie, you…"

"Look, I'll be out of here in a week. I can't afford to live here anymore anyway."

"Charlie…"

"Grow a fucking pair Henry."

I shake my head, shut the door, and phone a local rental office.

. . . .

When she opens the door, she has blonde hair. I tell her as much.

"What happened to your eye?" she asks.

"I, ah—I accidentally sold a bum pack of baseball cards to the son of a very angry, very strong Vietnam Vet."

"Oh…"

"Yeah."

"So, you're like—a counterfeit baseball card dealer?"

"Formerly, although it might actually be a metaphor for something a little more contemptable."

"Don't you mean an allusion?"

"Maybe. There are a lot of holes in my writing."

"So now you're a…"

"Struggling novelist."

"Well—you know, I've never really dated a struggling novelist before."

"Well, you know, neither have I."

"Well, I like the eye. It makes me wish I hadn't changed my hair. We could have matched…"

We go downtown and wander around beneath the shadows of old brick buildings. I buy Gretchen a cup of coffee, and we visit my favorite used bookstore.

Gretchen finds a bizarre book of dolls put together almost as a punk rock poetry scrapbook; the expressions on the plastic faces write a litany of thoughts in my mind even before I read the headings, and the ensuing stories that validate everything button eyes or odd tattered arms or geometrically impossible positions ever could.

She also finds an old auction book filled with paintings done by virtually every noteworthy artist of the first half of the twentieth century. We sit on the shabby, burnt red carpet of the second floor staircase, staring at each page as if we were both five, and the pages contained pictures of our Christmas presents.

I'm trying not to become too enamored with her too quickly—I'm trying not to look too far into her too-silver eyes. I'm trying not to hang sweet, grinning pictures of our unborn children on her heavy bottom lip. I'm trying not to make floor plans on the delicate slope of her thin, white neck.

I put the ring back in my pocket and pick up a couple of dusty paperbacks.

We head to a large two-story antique store, and I immediately fall over in front of a crate of records. Ten minutes later, I look back up into the world. A girl, maybe sixteen, walks by with a woman I presume is her mother.

"Look, honey, maybe they have some old punk records."

"Psshhhhhhhh."

I climb two stairs, and find Gretchen immersed in odd, old clothes, staring off in the direction of a small arrangement of dolls.

"I like them."

"I've noticed."

"No—I mean—I collect them." She pauses and whispers, and her eyes get a little bigger, and a hint more devilish, "they have to be especially creepy though."

We climb through endless corners of things— things which have no place in this world, but to appear here at this moment and give off the general impression that you are walking through your grandparent's door and digging through all the trunks in their attic. There are, besides the records and books that predictably fascinate me, an innumerable amount of dinner trays, tables, hotel room paintings, ornate drinking glasses, racks of peculiar clothes, racially offensive wooden signs, chess sets, impossible musical instruments, dusty mirrors, polished silver things in cases and old dolls.

I stand close by each time she spots one, or a pair, or an uneven family and watch her expression flip through channels of amusement, befuddlement, and impossible glee. She sells it so well, that it all starts to become contagious.

She finds a bum doll complete with rail yard pants and a five o'clock shadow and I know it's love.

"Oh, I have to buy this."

She tugs on doll clothes, and inspects leg writing and changes the light and angle of each one in her hand until she finds things that feel like home. She's an odd sort of scientist; she probably couldn't explain the process, just like an old war hero couldn't tell you why his leg tells you its raining—it just does. She is sure of these things. They are unmistakably transparent in her expressions.

I don't know why I find it so charming—so captivating—but I can tell it's raining somewhere.

There are moments in odd corners where we are close enough to wonder other things. I wonder what her tongue tastes like.

"Copper?"

All the clocks around us stop and watch to see what happens.

. . . .

I am rolling a thousand things over in my mind. It's all a little like sprinting through a giant museum; I can't catch anything long enough to make any sense. There's too much. It's all going too fast.

It's 3 a.m. again, and this time I'm standing on top of a mountain of boxes. My entire life is wrapped in cardboard—books, journals, pictures, letters, voodoo dolls, passports, pillow cases—everything.

A thin film of paper dust hangs in the air, catching the blue light like stars. I light a cigarette and watch it all dive into the ground. Galaxies parachute and perish into sad yellowing carpet fibers.

I wonder how many planets are living in my lungs? I wonder what rocket ship will carry all this out, and to where. I wish I had the script. I wish I'd bought the better remote, and could hit fast forward, skip, next, roll credits. I wish I were sitting on a leather sofa somewhere with central air, watching the bonus features.

Instead, I'm sweating like an overweight porn star, surfing boxes in the dead middle of the night, wishing up impossibilities while the death rattle of countless unknown civilizations hums on, unfazed, beneath me.

I reach up, and start to unscrew the last of the light bulbs.

. . . .

Eve pulls into the driveway and gets out, shaking her head.

"Rough day at the office, sis?"

"Let me tell you," she tells me.

I stand up and wait while she checks the mail and unlocks the front door.

Inside, we open a bottle of wine. I think about telling her all the things I'm thinking about, but I can't find a real, central, fixed point to start with; I can't hold a thought long enough to translate it all from the colossal unlinguistic vibration of sensory imaging back into English. So I say nothing.

We put on a movie and sit in utter silence, watching things spin around.

I catch myself in the middle of my own awkward, transparent expressions. I wonder if people can read anything into the broken, expectant smile, the bowed head, the eyes that expand a little when I breathe, or that look slightly down and to the right when I'm feeling guilty?

I trace parts of Eve's mantle: It's white inside of a yellow plaster frame. I think of standing up to explore the texture through my fingers.

Eve hits pause and excuses herself to the bathroom.

I spin the wheel and stick my finger randomly into the spokes. Start here. She comes in and sits back down.

"So I—uh—I saw Gretchen today. We went thrift store hopping, sort of exploring downtown. She's really—she's—she's not bad."

"Good for you."

"Yeah. Yeah, I'm going to see her again in a couple of days. Her hair's blonde now."

"Ugh, Watson was such an ass around her the other night. I wanted to smack him..."

"Yeah. I almost did. He walked into my room yesterday, grinning, and I almost threw a fucking chair at him."

"Yeah. I heard there was an *exchange*."

"Did you? That's a nice way to put it."

"He deserved it."

"Yeah, well. I guess Henry doesn't agree with you. I woke up this morning on a stack of boxes."

"I heard about that too."

"Yeah..."

"I'm sorry..."

"Ah, it's all right. I went by a rental office today, filled out an application, and checked out a few one-bedroom apartments. It'll be good for me, I think..."

"What are you going to do about work Charlie?"

"Are we going to talk about that too?"

I look down. Eve doesn't interrupt me looking down. We sit in utter, horrified silence.

"Look—I—ah..."

"Oh, Charlie, I know what you do. You could have said something." She tears up a little. "You didn't…"

"Oh, God, Eve—I'm—I'm sorry. I just didn't…"

"What?"

"I don't know." I try to look at her. She shakes her head. I look slightly off to the right. "I didn't want you to think I was turning into—I don't know…"

"What—my asshole dad, who lost everything, including his family, and his freedom for doing almost the exact same thing?"

"Uh—yeah. Him."

"You could have told me."

I shake my head, "I couldn't. I just couldn't for some reason. I—look, it's—it's not something I'm exactly proud of. It's not even something I spend a lot of time or thought on…"

"That's for sure."

"Look—I—it's not like I even actively went out and tried to move the stuff. I mean, I didn't print business cards or anything. It's just been a few close friends. It's been quiet. I've played it pretty safe."

"Except for last week when you got strangled? How many times did something like that happen? Did it ever occur to you that there are consequences for your actions?"

"Christ…"

"You know—it doesn't even matter. It doesn't matter how *safe* you play it. If you got caught, it wouldn't matter how quiet you were *trying* to be."

"Yeah. I—I know."

I stare through the mantel. I am yellow plaster crashing to the floor.

Eve keeps talking. I listen with my head bowed. Sometimes I nod. Sometimes I bite my tongue.

Eventually, I stand up and motion for the door.

"Look, Charlie, you're my best friend and…"

"I know. I'm—I'm sorry I didn't talk to you about it sooner. I'm sorry I didn't tell you."

"Yeah, well, it's not like I didn't know."

"I'm sorry…"

"Why? Why didn't you just get a job, like every normal person…"

"Because I'm *not* every normal fucking person. I've *never* fucking been every normal fucking person."

"You know what I mean. Charlie, it's not that hard…"

"But it is! It really fucking is! I don't know why I do the things I do—why I get lost listening to the rhythm of my heartbeat, wondering if I can make it stop by worrying about it stopping—I just do. And everything just becomes too difficult. Everything becomes blinding and impossible, and the world gets ten degrees hotter and I fall over when someone asks me where the bathroom is.

"This was the only thing I *could* do. I mean, I can write books that don't sell, and I can pretend I'm optimistic after pawning off two copies on drunks in a bar in the city every now and then, or I can make ten times that with a tenth of the work. It kept me in pretend optimistic land for a while. It kept me free."

"Well, that's just a great way to approach the world, Charlie, I'm real proud of you for all your freedom."

"I…" I look up at the ceiling and study something that probably isn't really there. "I tried to keep you

238

away from it. But it's over now, and I'll figure something else out. I always do. And it's better this way. I know that now."

I put my arms around her and tell I'm sorry.

"I love you, sis."

"I love you too, Charlie. You're my best friend. Just talk to me next time. Please?"

"I will. I promise."

I drive off.

. . . .

In the morning, I move all my things into storage before anyone is awake. I leave my key on the counter. I close the door. I don't look back.

I buy two cups of coffee, and make the three-hour drive to my mother's house.

She offers to let me stay in the empty bedroom of her old house in Alton until they sell it. I am hesitant, but I accept.

At night, I sit on a little bed in a not-so-little room in an anything-but-little house, cupping a small white pill to my lips. I swallow.

I want everything to stop spinning. I want everything to stop spinning. I want everything too— everything is spinning. Everything is spinning. I want everything.

. . . .

When I get back at midnight on Tuesday I walk up the winding sidewalk to the front door and walk into a mansion of steam.

I have one small suitcase of clothes and a laptop and I tell myself this is all I'll ever really need.

. . . .

Graham and I sit at the last two empty barstools in the entire state. It's so crowded, people have actually started dancing.

"Have you ever seen anything like this?"

"Not while I was sober."

"Hey, that sounds like a challenge. What do we have to do?"

"Well, I find alcohol can be quite calming in these situations."

"Heh. I remember being calm. All right Graham, you're on. I'll even trade you the first round for a cigarette."

"Fuck, I have a whole pack, help yourself."

"Thanks."

I shoot a flare gun over the bar and order a round of rum and cokes.

"Hey, I never got a chance to ask you. Did you ever talk to that girl Piera?"

"No. Man—I'm getting to old for that shit. And here's the thing—I know girls like that. I've even *dated* girls like that, and all they ever want to do is party and screw around and cop an attitude about it, and I'm just not in the mood anymore. I just have to be patient and rational, and I have to meet some girl my own age. And *then* it might have a snowball's chance in New Jersey."

"You know Piera's only five years younger than you."

"Yeah, but that's almost a quarter of her life."

"You'll be fine."

"Yeah. I think so. I think we'll all be fine, man. I mean, I know you've gone through some shit yourself."

"You heard?"

"This town is five people wide. Everybody hears everything. But I have to say, I think you've handled everything pretty well."

"So far…"

. . . .

When she opens the door, her hair is purple. I tell her as much.

"Damnit, Charlie! Your bruise is green now. I thought we'd match."

"If you like, I can run into something."

"No that's okay. Maybe I have a sweater…"

We drive around until we find a little village of used furniture stores cornered by the runoff of train tracks.

"I need an end table," she tells me, hopping out of the car with a bright smile and skipping like a child.

I dig through a few small piles of records by the door, while she streaks incandescent lights through the thin alleys between old dusty furniture in the dim light.

Upstairs, we find a rapping Santa doll dressed in black leather biker clothes with frills still in the box. We both pause. I reach out slowly to press the "test" button. It sways and raps awkwardly.

"I think I'm in love."

"He's pretty great."

241

"Yeah. I think I get the doll fascination now," I say, laughing.

Gretchen twists her head sideways at me, then smiles. Everything slows down a little.

Back downstairs, she haggles the shopkeeper down eight dollars on a ten dollar end table and celebrates by buying me a book and picking up a small ghost-eyed doll for herself.

I take her to a little café where we order martinis with pretentious names, along with sandwiches and a little plate of fruit and cheese. She's just had a tooth pulled, and is cutting everything into narrow slices to fit through the thin, slightly swollen slit of her jaw. I wince a little with each bite she takes, but it's not so much of a hardship as it is another odd endearment to add to her growing collection.

After a second drink, in a bit of a blur, we drive to yet another thrift store just down the road.

Inside, she unearths another dark corner filled with the little orphan minions of her addiction. I stand, and watch her paw over plastic hair and tiny polyester gowns, looking for clues towards birth dates or the fingerprints of past owners.

A large vase falls over at her side, shattering instantly. She freezes a laugh and backs away slowly. A clerk rushes over and picks up the shards.

"Should I offer to pay?" I whisper at her side, cupping my own laughter.

"Not—yet..."

We circle the store slowly, backwards, and disappear, laughing.

I buy a bottle of port on the way back to her house.

Inside, her little dog barks at me like a miniature fire truck. I crouch on the floor and offer it a stuffed giraffe. It turns its little head sideways, then lunges forward happily into my lap.

Gretchen smiles at me as if I were the creepiest doll yet.

"Let's see what's on," she says as she plops down on the couch in the middle of the room. She yawns a little, but realizes she can't open her mouth too wide, and winces and squints her too-silver eyes. I sit down next to her and furl a concerned eyebrow. She laughs at me, and the world slows down.

I think I can almost see her thoughts—I pick them out of the air, and arrange an imaginary bouquet of wildflowers.

I have another glass of port. She does the same.

Between movies I won't remember later, I kiss the thin slit of her slightly swollen jaw. Then her lips. Then her forehead.

Her fingers find my fingers. She leans back into me, and I hold her there, perfectly still, perfectly numb, perfectly and imperfectly matched in her own abnormal world of injuries and art and obsession with finding everything that's ever been irrevocably lost.

I find something in the upper right hand corner of her left eye, and I take a walk with it into the back of her mind.

"Copper?" it asks.

"No. She tastes like Gretchen."

The clock spins off its axis. We sit still, our hands locked, our eyes half-closed. Everything is numb and tingling all at the same time.

"Do you want to stay here tonight?" she finally asks, craning her neck towards the rising curl of my lips, joining both together through the thin slit of light hanging in the living room.

"Yes."

. . . .

In the morning, her hair is purple. I tell her as much.

She rolls over, puts her head neatly on my shoulder, and reaches for my left hand, locking our fingers together. My right hand traces the soft skin of her back, just below her shoulders.

And for once, I'm not really studying any of this. I already know what color her wall is, and that her hair smells like grapes and coconuts, and how many steps it takes to get to the bathroom in the dark. For once, I just close my eyes and settle against this lovely little thing settling against me, and the world slows down, and we with it.

Later, I do manage to get up and drive back to my mother's soon to be former house to get cleaned up and take care of a few of the ten thousand new loose ends the world has dropped off on my now-nonexistent doorstep.

I call the rental office. My application has gone through, and I am approved for just enough to rent a small hole inside another hole inside a wall.

I take a deep breath, and turn the shower just right of scalding. I get in the thin stall, crouch down, and let the water run over me.

. . . .

It's the 4th of July. Gretchen and I drive to a nearby fairground to catch a free fireworks show. She holds my right hand in her lap as I drive. I look over and see her smiling. She looks less devilish now than she does peaceful. I try to watch the road.

We sit over a concrete wall, and let our legs dangle over a small creek while several sad fireworks sputter out and die. The crowd around us gasps, is let down, sighs, and wanders off.

"Come on, I'll buy you a funnel cake," I tell her.

We walk in perfect time together, wandering the fairground, past the tilt-a-whirl, through the ice cream stands, and towards the sweet smell of sugary, burnt dough.

I tug at her chin a little and kiss her. We stand there motionless for a moment.

"Charlie?"

I blink and look straight ahead, "Yeah?"

"You know I'm yours, don't you?"

I want to say something as beautiful and as concise as those six words which are now running down my spine, making everything numb and lovely and dizzying.

I look at her too-silver eyes, and know that they are serious; they are floating in space, backed by water, running through my insides, and dissolving all previous means of boy girl pretense and rendering the world still, finally.

I run my fingers through the back of her hair and kiss her until God himself gives up and turns out all the lights.

. . . .

I spend the next day wandering the long, fragrant suburban backyard with Tim and his last pack of baseball cards. He shows me his Prince Fielder rookie card.

"This is about the last of it, Charlie."

"Heh. I'm all out too."

"Yeah. I think I'm going to quit when this is gone. I think it's actually starting to get in the way."

"Well, good for you man."

"Yeah. I mean—we'll see."

"Yeah. Whatever you do, you're meaning to do well. I think that's as important as anything. You know? You might fuck up and regress and do this fucked up thing or that fucked up thing. We're human. That happens. It always does. It's as unavoidable as gravity."

"Yeah…"

"But you really mean to get it right. You always have."

"Yeah. I do..."

"I've noticed. You know, I'm kind of proud of us lately. I think we're doing all right."

"Well, that remains to be seen…"

Tim tells me about another girl he's going after. He excuses himself when she calls, and I can hear him mumbling and see him gesturing awkwardly on the back porch as if she was right there.

I sit inside checking emails from my publisher. I have to send five more copies out today for prospective distributors. I write down the addresses.

Tim opens the door.

"How'd it go?"

"All right, I suppose. I guess we're doing something tomorrow. What the fuck is there to do in this down? I don't even remember."

"Heheh. You can always take her thrift store hopping, then out for a martini."

"Hey, that's not bad…"

We wander around the backyard for a little while talking about all the possibilities being born around us. I cut off a few flowers here and there for Gretchen. I think I read somewhere that girls like that sort of thing.

. . . .

We're sitting, Gretchen and I, on a small wooden dock, watching the nascent sunset sink into a still body of black water. Her little dog is dancing over us, leaping back and forth across a small of a parade of picnic tables at our backs. Everything else in the world has finally begun to slow down.

I have her—I have moments like this one that seem to repeat without skipping. I have a new book to sell, and the bus to New York runs back and forth at least three times a day. I have some real chances. I have actually managed to hustle my way away from hustling into a relatively honest—and disarmingly hopeful—set of circumstances.

I almost begin to question exactly how everything happened, where everything went, and where I'm really going with all this. But why? Why do I always have to dissect every seemingly innocent circumstance until I've distilled away all the mystery, all the unexplainable beauty and hushed pause, and boil everything away until all thats left is a terrifying ring of finality? Why?

Why?

I don't know what's going to happen in a year. I don't know what's going to happen in a week. I honestly don't have even the slightest idea how I got here, but for the moment—for this moment—everything around me seems real and well met and possible.

And we sit here, Gretchen and I, a pair of uncertain angels living under the blue banner of heaven, wondering: What will happen next?

. . . .

CPSIA information can be obtained at www.ICGtesting.com
Printed in the USA
BVOW020358260712

296085BV00001B/1/P